I0712313

FOREVER MY LOVE

Forever My Love
Copyright © 2022 by MW Dacosta.

All rights reserved. No part of this publication may be reproduced, distributed, or transmitted in any form or by any means, including photocopying, recording, or other electronic or mechanical methods, without the prior written permission of the copyright owner and the publisher, except in the case of brief quotations embodied in critical reviews and certain other noncommercial uses permitted by copyright law. For permission requests, write to the publisher, addressed "Attention: Permissions Coordinator," at the address below.

ARPress
45 Dan Road Suite 5
Canton MA 02021

Hotline: 1(888) 821-0229
Fax: 1(508) 545-7580

Ordering Information:

Quantity sales. Special discounts are available on quantity purchases by corporations, associations, and others. For details, contact the publisher at the address above.

Library of Congress Control Number:		2024903345
ISBN-13:	Softcover	979-8-89356-281-1
	eBook	979-8-89356-280-4

Printed and bound in The United States of America.

FOREVER MY LOVE

M W Dacosta

ARPress
ILLUMINATING IDEAS
EMPOWERING VOICES

Dedication

To all who believe in the power of true love

Introduction

Is it possible to lose love and find it again years later? For many of us, true love seems to escape us. We have all fallen in love with someone whom we thought we could spend the rest of our lives with, only to have our hearts crushed and all our dreams evaporate before our eyes.

I believe that true love can be found, although at times it seems that we may be searching in vain. We should never give up hope because sometimes just when we think that it is never going to happen, it does.

Maureen had been betrayed by her first love, and even though she tried to love again, it was not the same.

Anthony, in spite of trickery and deceit, held on to his dream to be reunited with his one true love. If only she knew how much he loves her and wants to make her his. If only she would give him a second chance.

Just like our two lovers, we too have to believe and be willing to take a chance allowing our hearts to lead the way. When you find your true love, you will be able to say without any hesitation,

Forever my love.

Chapter 1

The alarm clock rang; I reached over to turn it off. It always seems like every time, just when I am settling into the sweetest sleep, that stupid clock jars me awake. Oh well, time to get up. It was 6:45 a.m. I lay there, my eyes looking around my bedroom. I turned my head to look at the man lying next to me. His eyes were closed; I knew he was awake, just pretending to be asleep. I wondered, *what had happened to us?* Before, mornings like these would have found him holding me close. His arms would be around me, and he would be kissing my neck and my back.

I have been in this relationship with James for the past three and half years. I had hoped that by now we would have been married. We had decided to move in together, as it didn't make sense for us to be paying rent for two apartments when we spent so much time together in one of the apartments.

About fourteen months ago, we had made the decision to move into my apartment, which was nearer to public transportation, and a smaller nonelevator building. The neighborhood was not bad either with a tree-lined street and a large park just two blocks away. I felt that the move was like a prelude to marriage. I thought that it gave both of us a chance to see how well we would live together.

My mother always said that there is an old adage that says "visit me" and 'live with me' are two different things.'" My mom had all these sayings that she would quote to us as a situation arose.

At first, I felt like I was in seventh heaven; I felt we made such a perfect couple. Now, recently I have been wondering what was causing us to drift apart.

There was a time when we couldn't get enough of each other. We would get home from work, and before we ate dinner, we would be all over each other, our passion fueled by being away from each other all day at work.

James had been so romantic, especially when we first got started. I awoke many mornings to his hands caressing my body; we could make love, and he would say the sweetest sensual things. Our lovemaking was great, but as time went on, I began to notice that some little incidents would eventually escalate into a shouting match, leaving us both feeling hurt and upset.

I snapped out of it and got out of the bed. I went into the bathroom and did the usual morning routine—take a shower, brush my teeth, wash my face, and apply all the toiletries that most women use. I looked at myself in the full-length mirror. "Maureen," I said to myself, "*girl, you are getting old.*" I was twenty-eight years old, and I worried if I would get married and be able to have a son or a daughter for that matter. I thought myself attractive; I was five feet five inches, and I weighed 130 pounds, and I tried to keep my body in shape by walking daily.

I was interrupted suddenly as James knocked on the door and said,

"Maureen, are you going to stay in here all morning? I have to get in there too."

"Sorry, babe, I guess I am losing track of time."

I put on my robe and went into the kitchen; James had already put the kettle on to boil. I made us two cups of tea. We both drank tea instead of coffee; occasionally, I would enjoy a cup of Joe, but I am a tea baby.

We never made breakfast before going to work on weekdays; it was just too rush, and we didn't have the time to enjoy it. Plus, over the years having practiced myself to eating later in the morning, I had no appetite to eat so early anyhow. What we did on mornings instead was to pick up breakfast on our way into the office and ate it here. I took my cup of tea with me to the bedroom as I went into the closet to select a suit to wear.

I chose a royal-blue skirt suit and got dressed. I love skirt suits or dresses. I never wear pants or pantsuits to work. Call me old fashioned, but I think a woman looks more feminine in a skirt or a dress. Don't get me wrong, that's just my opinion and my choice; I just like to look as feminine as I can. I chose a blue floral scarf to go around my neck and a brooch for my lapel. I always took care to coordinate my outfits, an effort that usually pays off by the compliments I receive.

I am sure my coworkers think I spend my whole paycheck buying clothes. Nothing, however, could be further from the truth. I shop the outlet stores. Sometimes I would go to Connecticut or New Jersey to the outlets to shop. You will be surprised when you see the prices of some of the designer suits. The same suit at any of the big stores would cost you figuratively an arm and a leg.

As I finished my dressing and my tea, I picked up my handbag and headed for the door.

"I am leaving, James," I said. "I will give you a call later."

"OK," he replied through the door. "Have a great day. I will talk to you later."

I walked out, slammed and locked the door behind me, and began my daily two-and-a-half block walk to the subway.

Every day on the subway is an adventure waiting to happen. I must admit in the weeks and months following 9/11, I dreaded coming to the city. Anytime I came home from college, I was fearful of getting on the subway for fear of a terrorist attack. I tried to avoid the subways for a long time until I finally graduated and had to go to work.

I had gotten a job in Manhattan, so I had no choice but to get on the subway. Now, 2009, it has been eight years since that horrible day. I still get nervous thinking about it.

I don't believe I will ever forget that day; upon hearing the news of the planes crashing in the World Trade Center, I was terrified for my parents, especially my father who worked in Manhattan for a delivery service. At any given time, he could be in any part of Manhattan from uptown to downtown. My mother was a social worker also and did some work in Manhattan on occasions.

I remember frantically trying to get through to them on my cellphone. When I finally got a hold of my mother, she was fine and she had heard from Dad and he was fine and on his way home. Luckily for me, my family was safe, and I was so thankful that nothing had happened to them.

For days and weeks, as details emerged, I am sure, like many New Yorkers and people around the world, I was in a state of shock. Even now as I take the subway daily, the thoughts of a terrorist attack still linger in the back of my mind.

Taking the subway, to me, is always a study in human behavior and body language, not to mention that you can never be sure if the trains are running on schedule or whether we will be delayed because of train traffic ahead or a sick passenger. Some days, my twenty-five-minute commute turns into forty or forty-five minutes.

While I know that New York City has the best subway system in the world (my opinion, of course; after all, I am a native New Yorker), some days, my commute is quiet enough that I can read a book or a magazine; and other days, there is someone preaching, calling sinners to repent; and still there are other days when the homeless come on begging for money.

I have seen people with so many afflictions, some so dirty and smelly, that my heart goes out to them. Then I have to deal with the youngsters on the way to school who talk loudly, teasing each other and challenging each other to mock fights and petty augments. I guess this is what makes New York City the greatest city in the world.

As you listen to the different accents, New York is truly, as they say, "a melting pot." If you have a keen ear and some background knowledge, you can differentiate the Bajans from the Guyanese, the Jamaicans from the Vincentians, and all the islands in between.

Truth is, I love New York, with all its diversity and craziness. Today, as I got on the subway, I was able to get a seat, and I pulled out a small book of daily inspirational writing and started to read it. Before I knew it, I was at Hoyt Street, my stop. I got up quickly, and exited the train.

I came out the subway and onto the street. There is a little restaurant that I usually stop by daily and pick up whatever breakfast I felt like. As I step in the door, Joe or Marty would always say to me,

"How you doing today, Maureen? What can we fix for you?" I always returned their greeting, and whatever I order was ready quickly, as they just knew I was on my way to work and time was of the essence.

Today, as usual, the guys greeted me, and I ordered a toasted corn muffin, lightly buttered, and a cup of tea. They knew me so well; I didn't have to tell them how I like my tea; they knew—tea with milk and one and a half sugar. My order was handed to me; I wished the guys a great day and headed off to the office.

As I made my way into the building, I was thinking about our upcoming audit and the fact that I wanted to review some of our files to make sure everything was in order. I was also later in the morning, to sit in on an interview for a new fiscal person. Our fiscal person had handed in her resignation three weeks ago. She found a better position with a firm in the city. I was sorry to see her go, but I understand that we each have to follow our own career path.

On her last day, we all got together and bought her a farewell gift of a lovely pair of gold earrings. I ordered some buffalo wings with coleslaw and potatoes salad along with an assortment of juices, and we had a small send-off party for her.

Over the past two weeks, I have reviewed about ten resumes for the position and had identified three candidates that I felt we should interview. Today will be the first of the three interviews, which were scheduled for today and tomorrow.

The candidate that we would be interviewing today sounded very promising; she has worked for another nonprofit organization in Queens.

Of course, everyone tries to make themselves look good through their resume. Meeting with them and talking to them usually reveal facets of their personality that cannot be captured in their resume.

As usual, many days, I am always the one who is first to arrive in the office. I like to be early; it gives me the chance to settle myself and have my breakfast before starting my day. Our executive director Steven also arrives early. As management, it is so important that we set the standard for our employees so that they know that tardiness is not acceptable.

"Good morning, Maureen," Steven said as he walked in the office.

"Good morning, Steven. How are you today?"

"I'm here thanking God for waking me up this morning. I got a call from Miller, Green, and Cohen yesterday. The auditors will be here Monday morning at nine o'clock. Have you been able to finish reviewing our files to make sure everything is current and up to date?"

"Not quite finished. I plan to work on that today and tomorrow, so Monday morning, we will be ready."

"I know I can count on you to get it done. If you need help with anything, let me know. You could probably use Keisha to help with any filing or copying of documents. I want everything to be right when the auditors get here. An excellent audit means funding for us because donors will see that we use funds as they have been allocated.

"I hear that, and I will make sure everything is ready when they walk in here Monday morning. Don't forget we have the interview at eleven o'clock today."

"Oh yeah, I will be ready. I have the resume in my office. I will look it over one more time, and when she comes, call me and I will come out to meet her."

"OK, will do."

I returned to my office. I have my work cut out for me. I understand what Steven was saying; if we hope to continue to receive funding so we could expand into the other boroughs, we have to be transparent in all that we do.

As we move forward, we are planning to tackle some of the big-named corporations with the hope of receiving grants from them. Currently, most of our funding comes from the state. I was able to get some funds from one of the city agencies, whose goal is to relocate woman and children out of the shelter system and in to their own apartment. We have a meeting scheduled with the city councilman for this area, who has expressed his interest in the work that we are doing.

We were thrilled when he stopped by at our open house and promised the resources of his office to assist us in whatever capacity they could help. Hopefully, with his help, we will be able to see what other city agencies may be able to help fund some of the programs we plan to institute.

Right now, however, replacing our fiscal person was key, and we wanted to find that person who will be willing to work and become part of our family here. We need a team player who understands that we all are working toward one goal of providing housing services for New Yorkers. It is our commitment and our belief that all people are entitled to decent and affordable housing.

I set about working on my project; before I knew it, Keisha was buzzing to say that Ms. Wilson was here for the interview. I put on my jacket that I had removed, buttoned it all way, picked up the phone, and buzzed Steven.

I walked to the reception area just as Steven came out of his office and joined us.

"Good morning, Ms. Wilson. I am Maureen Coleman. I had spoken to you when we set up the appointment. This is our director, Steven White. Welcome."

I extended my hand and shook her hand, with Steven doing the same.

"Thank you, Ms. Coleman, Mr. White. Good morning."

"If you will follow us, Ms. Wilson, we will be meeting in the conference room."

With that, I turned and began my walk, followed by Ms. Wilson, with Steven bringing up the rear.

For the next twenty minutes, we spoke and learned quite a bit about our candidate; she had a good sense of how the not-for-profit organizations worked. She was definitely qualified, having a BS in accounting and planning to work toward her master's in finance in the fall. At the end, we thanked her for coming, and we told her she should hear from us by next week. We did let her know that we had two others to interview, and we will inform her once we had completed our interviews.

As the day came to a close, I was debating whether to work an extra hour this evening, as tomorrow, I wanted to leave on time. I had Diane's birthday party on Saturday, and I wanted to finalize my outfit. I decided to spend the extra hour and work on making sure I didn't have to stress myself out when the auditors came.

I picked up the phone, and I called James to let him know I will be a little late this evening. He said OK, that he too may be late, as he was contemplating stopping at the gym to work out. *Oh well, I guess that settles that!* I wondered if he would have called me to say something. He never called all day today. Before, I could have expected at least two calls just to see how my day was going.

Is the writing on the wall for us? *"Maureen,"* I said myself, *"Please stop. You are over thinking again. Don't you have work to do?"* I snapped out of it and turned to the pile of papers on my desk. *"Let's do this,"* I said softly, and I started working.

Chapter 2

TGIF. I was really happy that it was Friday; I was looking forward to the weekend. We had an invitation to my friend Diane's birthday party on Saturday evening.

When I received her invite, I wondered how come she decided to have a birthday party; this was not a milestone birthday for her. I believe that we were the same age. Knowing Diane as I do, it didn't surprise me, she just loves to entertain. She is someone who doesn't need an occasion to have a party; she plans and many times just have a soiree for the fun of it.

As I left work on Friday, I felt that I had accomplished my task of making sure our files were in order for the audit on Monday. I stopped by a little store, which was two blocks away from my job, that carried a wide variety of unusual costume jewelry. I wanted a necklace and earring set to complement my dress for the party.

I always look for pieces of jewelry that have that uncommon look to them. Many times, someone would come up to me and asks, "Where did you get that? It is so unusual," or they may make a comment as to how beautiful what I was wearing looked.

Everyone in the store knew me well. Usually, I would wait for Marie to assist me; I felt that she gave me her honest opinion and did not try to convince me to make a purchase just to get a sale. She always kept any nice pieces that were recently bought in so I could get first pick of the new merchandise.

Today, I was eyeing a gold choker with matching earrings and bracelet. The choker would be perfect to accentuate my neckline, as my dress was off the shoulders. I found just what I was looking for, and I purchased it, feeling quite satisfied that I had everything I needed to look great for the party.

As I arrived home, I received a call from James to say that he was out with some of his coworkers for a drink and he would be in later. I said OK, but within, I was recalling how many Friday nights we started our weekend off with dinner. We loved to go to City Island. James was crazy about seafood, especially crab legs, which he would refer to as 'crab toes'.

There were about three restaurants on the island that we frequented regularly. For us, all we needed was a table for two with white tablecloth, fresh flowers and we would eat and laugh and just enjoy each other's company.

Stop worrying, Maureen, I told myself. *Everything is going to be all right.*

I miss those days; as much as I tried to console myself, I knew that there was a change in our relationship. Most Friday nights recently, have found me alone or having to occupy myself doing some chores in order to take my mind off of the change that I feel within our relationship. Even when we go out to eat lately, it is just not like it used to be.

Saturday evening came, and we got dressed for the party. Diane had asked all her guests to wear red and white with a touch of gold. The affair was semiformal, and I wore a red-and-white silk floral dress with red high shoes and red evening bag. I finished the look with the gold accessories I had bought yesterday.

Diane had the hall beautifully decorated. Red streamers hung from the ceiling. Red and white balloons were on each table. Three sections of the walls were decorated with sheer material designed in a draping effect with red and white lights that shone through the material. Whoever the decorator was, he or she had done a terrific job. There were red and white lights that wrapped around the room, and the tables were alternately covered with red and white tablecloths. Everything looked so elegant and very tastefully done.

We were seated, and the DJ started playing. I really felt happy to be here. I had known Diane since high school, and we were relatively close; we didn't talk every day or see each often, but our friendship was such that I felt that I could call anytime I needed someone to listen, and she knew the same was true for me where she was concerned.

Diane was married to a really nice guy; someone she had met three years ago. I must admit that I was surprised when she called to let me know that Joe had proposed to her. She met Joe after I had met James. Their romance took off like a wild fire, and I guess Joe wasted no time in setting his plans in motion. I was happy for her even though I thought that I would have walked down the aisle before her.

I have to admit that I am ready to get married and settled down. At twenty-eight years old, I could feel my biological clock ticking. I would love to have a baby, and while I know that women are able to have children into their forties, I want my baby while I was still young and have the energy that I know I would need to care of him. Boy or girl, it didn't matter; I just wanted one.

When I first started dating James, we had discussed our love of children, and I always felt that we would make great parents. Now I could almost feel the distance growing between us. We have gone from talking about marriage to "What's your hurry?"—he would say— "We'll get it together."

"Maureen,"—I heard James call my name; for a minute, my mind had wandered away from the party— "I am going to the bar to get a drink. Do you want your usual?"

"Sure, bring me Alizé and orange juice."

I sat back and looked around me; the room was filling up. Diane had a lot of friends, and she really was a great hostess. I caught a glimpse of her by the door, greeting her guests. She must have recently arrived, as she was not at the door when we came in.

She wore a slim-fitting red chiffon gown with a white sash that went around her waist and tied in the back into a big beautiful bow. Diane was a beautiful woman; she always carried herself well. She was a true fashion diva.

She had always like designing, made it her career. She has a small business where she designs and creates outfits for her clients. James returned with the drink and handed it to me.

"Diane sure knows how to throw a party," he said.

"She sure does," I replied.

The DJ had opened the floor for dancing, and we danced. As the evening wore on, I noticed on two different occasions James excused himself and walked over to a table on the opposite side of the room. He was talking to and danced with a woman. She looked about my height, very attractive, and I wondered who she was. I had never seen her before.

Eventually, dinner was served, and birthday greetings were given by some of the guests, and the party continued to 2:00 a.m. We took our leave of Diane and Joe, thanking them for a wonderful evening, and wished Diane a happy birthday.

As we started the drive home, I said to James, "Who was that woman you were talking to at the party?"

"She is a friend I have not seen in a long time."

"What's her name?" I asked.

"What is this, Maureen—" he fired back— "an inquisition? Her name is Linda. Anything else you want to know?"

"James," I said, "it's just that I have never heard you speak of her or seen her before."

"Maureen,"—his voice sound disgusted— "do you think I could tell you about all my friends? I am constantly meeting people and interacting with them, you know. I would really like to figure out what is your problem," he said.

"James," I replied, my voice low, "I do not want this to become a fight. You are taking this to a whole other level. This is just an innocent question on my part."

"Yeah, right," he said, "you seem as if you need to know every little detail of my life. I think you are insecure and are always looking for something to hold on to as something to hold over my head."

"James, "let's not fight over this. We had a lovely evening. Let's not spoil it by arguing. I am sorry. I didn't mean anything by my inquiry."

"You know what, Maureen," he said, "just forget it."

We rode the rest of the way home in silence. I thought to myself, this is what I am talking about. The smallest incident has the potential to spiral out of control. It was as if he is taking the opportunity to drive a deeper wedge between us.

We arrived home. I took a quick shower and removed my makeup. I put on my nightgown and got into bed. James seemed to linger long in the bathroom, and at one point, I could hear him in the kitchen. I believe he fixed himself a drink and sat at the dining table drinking it. He eventually came to bed and turned on his side, facing away from me. No good night kiss, no hug, and no pulling me close to lie in his arms. I lay on my back, wondering, what is happening here? What is wrong with me? I silently asked myself. Why cannot I find a man that wants to marry and settle down? What am I doing wrong?

Maureen, my inner voice said, stop! The right man will come along. Have some faith in yourself, but most of all, have faith in God and believe that he will send the right man at the right time. I remembered praying in my mind as I drifted off to sleep.

As I opened my eyes, the sunlight had started to fill my room. I had slept soundly. I don't remember waking up once as I sometimes do and look at the clock on the cable box. I think I was mentally and physically tired between the party and just dealing with James's hostility; my body saw sleep as a great escape to rest and rejuvenate.

Late spring is always the best time of year. The weather is almost perfect; not too hot like summer and not too cold like winter. As my eyes fully opened and I turned my head, I realized that James was not in the bed.

There was a sweet smell of breakfast cooking. Ah yes, it was Sunday morning, the day to sleep late and have a big breakfast. As I lay there thinking, James appeared at the bedroom door, a tray in his hand and a big smile on his face.

"Good morning, sunshine," he said. I know my face carried a look of pure surprise.

"Good morning," I replied. "What's happening?"

"I made you breakfast," he said. "What will it be, coffee, tea, or me?"

"Wow, some choices," I replied.

"Don't worry," he said, "you can have all three." He placed the tray over me. He had made scramble eggs with Canadian bacon, whole wheat toast, lightly buttered, and a cup of tea. A slice of melon with a few strawberries completed the meal.

"Thanks, James," I said. "I am surprised."

"Listen, Maureen," he said, "about last night, I am sorry. I got carried away. I did not mean to snap at you."

"Let's forget it, James," I replied. "Today is a new day."

"Let me get my plate."

With that, he left and returned with his tea and a plate of the same meal he served me.

We ate our meal, pretty much in silence, punctuated with a few remarks about last night's party. He suggested that maybe later today we could visit the Brooklyn Botanical Gardens. It sounded great; I had not been to the garden in a long time. I especially like the Japanese garden; that area has a very serene feel to it, calming and beautiful.

We finished breakfast, and I went to take a shower. The warm water cascading over my body felt so good. My mind drifted to a place that was warm and comfy. I was so caught up in that moment that I did not realize that James had joined me in the shower. I felt his arms go around my waist, and as I turned my head, his lips descended on mine. I was a little startled; we had not taken a shower together in months.

His lips on mine, his tongue in my mouth, the urgency of his kiss, it took me a minute to respond. This was the James of old, the one whose kisses set me on fire and started tingling sensations that ran down my chest into my belly and all between my legs, the kisses that started my natural juices flowing.

I returned his kiss, my lips kissing his neck and onto his chest. His hand cupped my breast. Bending his head, he sucked the nipple into his mouth, his tongue circling it. He let go of the breast and reached for my washcloth, squeezed the body wash onto it, and proceeded to rub the soapy cloth all over my body. He washed my back, between my legs, and all the way down to my feet. I in turn did the same thing to him, washing him the same way he washed me.

Just feeling the warm water falling over us, the passion of the moment, unleashed every emotion in my body. A soft sigh escaped my lips as his tongue traveling down my stomach unto my belly, kissing and licking the water as it fell on me.

We got out of the shower, our bodies wet, stopped long enough to dry some of the water off before walking into the bedroom and into the bed. The kisses continued, his lips all over my breast, sucking the nipples and turning me into a twisting, groaning woman who couldn't wait for him to enter me so that I could feel every move he made. I matched his moves, my body caught up in all the steamy, passionate love he was giving. He knows how I get, when I get wild.

"Girl, you are so sweet," he said. "Damn, I want this," he continued.

"It's all yours, baby," I whisper between sighs and my hips that were moving like crazy. I could feel my body start to go cold and that tingling sensation that just shot right through me, and he knew I had climaxed. He was not far behind me, from his movement and the cries that echoed from his lips,

"Maureen, baby, baby, oh god, baby," and the world exploded for him.

I have to admit making love to this man was great; to feel him in me, to look into his face as he made love to me, and to hear his cry leave me weak but satisfied.

He pulled me close and kissed me, his body and breathing returning to normal mode. He didn't speak, just held me close. As I lay in his arms, I was thinking even with all this love, I could feel a difference. After being in a relationship for a while, you learn a lot about the person you are intimate with, and sometimes you can sense the changes, no matter how subtle they may seem.

I love James, and I wanted this to work so badly. Maybe all these changes that I perceive are all in my mind. Who knows, I am probably making a mountain out of a mole hill. I lay there resolving to stop thinking so hard and let it all work out. He must still love me; after all, he still wanted to make love to me.

Chapter 3

Ha! Monday morning already; seems like it was just Friday. I sometimes wonder why the weekend goes by so quickly. Today, I actually dreaded going to work. Today was the start of our yearly audit.

I had made sure that everything was in order, and I was very proud of the fact that we had done very well on our last year's audit. I had no doubt that we would do just as well this year, but having the auditors around is always such a disruption of our daily routine.

Our organization existed on grants that we solicited. Writing requests for proposals was the main thing that I do. Audits are important, and I understood that, as it made our seeking funds a lot easier. Those foundations and agencies that were willing to fund us can rest assured that the money is used for the purposes intended.

Our organization is a not-for-profit housing advocacy group. We offer counseling for individuals with housing problems. We also referred clients to government agencies for additional help where needed. We sometimes act as an intermediary between clients and landlords.

We have a number of attorneys who offered pro bono services to our clients, advising them on a variety of issues. We have five full-time counselors who provide these services. Our executive director is Steven White, a man who had started out with community work in Brownville and the East New York area of Brooklyn. He is a seasoned community organizer who has worked his way through the ranks and has a reputation of being a man who can be trusted and has the community's best interest at heart.

After college, I went to work for a firm in Manhattan. I had met Steven at a fund-raiser two years earlier, and in talking to him, I was inspired to work for the betterment of our community and its people. I quit my job in Manhattan and assisted Steven in getting our organization up and running. My title says that I am the assistant executive director, that is, for the professional side of me; at heart, I am an organizer who want to see people given a fair shake, not shafted because they may be poor, uneducated immigrants who don't understands their rights, etc.—the list is long.

Alright, let me get off my soap box and back to the matter at hand. I had to leave home a little earlier than usual, as I wanted to be in the office early to make sure everything was in order. I wanted to have the coffee perked, and I planned to picked up some doughnuts and mini bagels for our auditors.

This morning, there was no time to play around. I had told James about the audit, so it was no surprise to him to see me up and getting out of the house. I took the train as usual and was in the building by 8:15 a.m. I checked to see that the cleaners had done a proper job of cleaning our small kitchen/lunchroom and the bathrooms. Of course, I was not surprised to see Steven walk in a few minutes behind me.

"Good morning, Maureen. I see you are on top of things as usual."

"You better believe it," I replied. "How was your weekend?" I asked.

"We took the kids to Queens to visit my mother. They stayed over Saturday night—gave Gloria and I a chance to go out to dinner and sleep late on Sunday. It was glorious."

"Oh, I envy you, those two adorable girls—can't wait to have some of my own."

"Trust me on this," he said. "Enjoy your freedom now you have it. Once those kids come along, you are mommy or daddy for the rest of your life."

"Like I said, can't wait."

Steven laughed and went into his office.

"Let me get my act together," he said as he turned and walked away.

By nine, all the staff were in, and as I sat at my desk, I expected the auditors from Miller, Greene, and Cohen to walk in anytime. I busied myself with the usual paperwork.

As I waited, I received a call from one of our clients named Mrs. Vickers. She was a seventy-five-year-old widow who was being harassed out of her apartment. She occupied a lovely three-bedroom apartment in Park Slope, in one of those turn-of-the-century buildings where the rooms were big and spacious. She was working with one of our counselors, but I had gotten to know her when she came in looking for help and was so concerned that she was going to become homeless after all those years of living in that building. She had raised her family there and was now all alone; her husband died two years ago, and her son and daughter had moved away and started their own families, one in Maryland and one upstate New York, in Albany.

As I was talking to her, Keisha buzzed me to say that the auditors were here and she had showed them into Steven's office. I told her I will be there shortly as soon as I got off the call.

I returned to Mrs. Vickers and promised her that I will continue our conversation in a little while. I told her I will call her back in about an hour. I had to assure her that I will call her back, as I could sense her being afraid and concern of being evicted for no other reason other than her apartment was rent stabilized and the ownership couldn't raise her rent to the prevailing rent for an apartment like hers.

I hung up the phone and walked over to Steven's office. As I walked in the door and to the side of Steven's desk, the two gentlemen who were seated stood up. Steven proceeded to introduce the men.

"Gentlemen," he said, "this is my assistant director, Maureen Coleman. Maureen, this is Mr. Ralph King and Anthony Bradley of Miller, Greene, and Cohen."

I extended my hand and shook Mr. King's hand and then Mr. Bradley's. Upon hearing the name and seeing Mr. Bradley, it took every ounce of strength I had in my body not to portray the shook I had on seeing Mr. Bradley.

Both gentlemen responded with "Good morning. Nice to meet you, Ms. Coleman," and resumed their seats.

I stood next to Steven as he asked me to set them up in our conference room so they could begin.

"Gentlemen," Steven said, "Ms. Coleman will be working with you directly and will provide you with all the files and data you will need."

"Thank you," they both replied.

"If you will show us the way, Ms. Coleman," Mr. King said, "we will go ahead and get started."

I walked out the room and told them to follow me. I showed them to the conference room, and Mr. King said, "Please give us a few minutes to get set up, and I will have a list of files we would like to begin with."

I told him that it was fine and, when they were ready, to call me at extension 119.

I walked out of the room as calmly as possible and headed quickly for the ladies' room. Once inside, I let my emotions take hold of me.

"I can't believe this, it's Tony. Oh god, this cannot be happening. How am I going to handle this?" I was beside myself. *"OK, Maureen, calm down,"* I told myself. *"You can handle this. Breathe and shake it out!"* I took a couple of deep breaths, I shook my body, and I calmly walked out of the ladies' room.

As I got back to my desk, Mr. King called to say he was ready with the list. *I can do this,* I repeated in my mind. *I can do this.* I went to the room and retrieved the list. Mr. Bradley was occupied setting up a desktop calculator and did not look in my direction as I interacted with Mr. King.

Fine, I thought to myself. He has it under control, so can I. Whatever you do, Maureen, don't make a fool of yourself.

I collected all the files that were asked for and delivered them to the conference room. I told Mr. King whenever he needed anything, to please feel free to buzz me. I returned to my office and called my best friend Lisa.

"Lisa, can we have lunch today? I have to talk to you."

"Sure, I go to lunch for 1:00 p.m. Is that, OK?" she replied.

"Yeah, that's fine. I'll meet you in front of your building at 1:00 p.m."

I returned Mrs. Vickers's call and chatted with her for a few minutes. I have to admit that I didn't really hear what she was trying to tell me. My mind kept drifting away as I was trying to reassure her that everything will be all right and that I will check with her counselor as to what progress has been made with her case. I couldn't wait for one o'clock.

The remainder of the morning went by uneventful. Mr. King had called for a few more files, and I had one of the counselors to offer them coffee and either a bagel or a donut. Mr. King had coffee and something to eat, but Mr. Bradley just had a cup of coffee.

At 12:50 p.m., I checked in with them to say I was about to go to lunch. Mr. King said that they were just thinking of doing the same thing. They said that they will be back within an hour. I said to both of them, "Enjoy your lunch."

I met Lisa, and we walked to a small pizzeria around the corner from her job, which was about two blocks away from mine on Bond Street. As we ordered a slice and sat down, I blurted out,

"Tony is here."

"Who are you talking about?"

"Tony, Tony Bradley," I replied angrily.

"Wait a minute, you mean your Tony Bradley, no! You lying."

"Yes, he is one of the auditors at my job right now."

"No, girl, you lying, for real? Are you serious?"

"For real, girl, as serious as a heart attack," I answered.

"Girl, what are you going to do?"

"Nothing. He's acting like he doesn't know me, so I am not going to show my ass and get insulted."

"Wow, this is some deep shit."

"I know. Lisa, right now, I am so torn up. I haven't seen this man in seven years, and today, he walks back into my life. Lisa, I took one look at him, and my knees started to shake. It took everything I had in me to compose myself and stand my ground."

"Girl, what are you going to do? After what he did to you, don't tell me you are still in love with this man."

"Lisa, I don't know. I am only telling you what happened to me. Lisa, my insides feel like jelly."

"Maureen, I should be a little more sensitive to your feelings. Listen to me, calm yourself. Everything is going to be all right. You can handle this. Call me tonight, and we will talk about it. I am here for you. Hey, remember I was there when it all went down. Girl, I got your back."

"Thanks, Lisa. I am not hungry. You can have my slice. I will call you tonight, OK?"

She got up and gave me a hug.

"You are going to be fine. Just be the professional woman that you are, and you will be all right."

We walked out, and we went our separate ways back to our offices. As I walked along, the beautiful weather outside was suddenly lost to me. Memorial Day will be next weekend, summer is coming, but suddenly, my world has turned into a winter's day as what happened between Anthony Bradley and I played in my mind.

I returned to the office, and the auditors had resumed their work after having lunch. The rest of the day passed by quickly, and before I knew it, it was 5:00 p.m.

Mr. King buzzed me to say that they were about to leave. I walked over to the conference room. Mr. King wanted to know if it was OK to leave everything as is until tomorrow. I assured him that the room would be locked and nothing will be tampered with. At that point, he said that he and Mr. Bradley will be leaving shortly. Just before turning to walk away, I wished them a good evening.

I couldn't wait to get home. As I got into the apartment, I undressed and sat on the bed thinking about the events of today.

My mind drifted back to 2001. I was in my second year of college at St. Mary's College, upstate New York. I needed help with math and decided to take some extra tutoring in the math lab. That's when I met Anthony Bradley. He would be graduating that June with his BS in accounting. He would graduate cum laude.

After a couple of sessions, I came to realize that this guy was brilliant. From all accounts, he just enjoyed solving mathematical problems and had a grasp of the subject that I wish I could have.

One afternoon as we were finishing up our session, he asked if I wanted to have a cup of coffee with him. I agreed, and we walked over to the cafeteria to get the coffee. I felt a little hungry, so I picked up an apple Danish to have with my coffee.

As I sat across from him, I was thinking to myself, *behind those glasses are a pair of beautiful eyes.* He was at least five feet nine or five feet ten, dark, slender built, his hair twisted but not dreadlock, quite good looking. We sat and talked about the beauty of math, as he called it, and how it really wasn't that complicated once you embraced it and not dread it. All in all, it was a very pleasant chat. As we parted ways, I found myself looking forward to the next time I would meet him.

My phone rang, and I jarred back to reality. It was Lisa.

"I thought you were going to call me as soon as you reach home."

"Yes, I was going to, but I came in and sat on the bed, and I drifted off into a daydream."

"Wake up, girl. We have things to talk about. So did he say anything to you when you went back to the office?"

"No," I replied, my mind flooded with all the thoughts of the day.

"Do you believe him? You mean he had not attempted to say a word to you about you two?"

"Nope, not a word. Well, it's his first day. Who knows, maybe he's just as shook at seeing me as I am at seeing him."

"Shock or no shock, he needs to say something," Lisa said, sounding so annoyed. "Girl, I could never forgive him if it was me, and as for Robin, if I saw her, I wouldn't even look in her direction. Tony was bad, but I blame Robin the most. She was your friend—hell, we were all friends. How could she do what she did to you if she was your friend?"

"Lisa, to this day, I have not been able to figure out what really happened. All I knew is that Tony was my boyfriend, and the next thing I know, he married Robin and had a kid. In all the times we have all been together, I never saw a sparkle of interest in Tony towards Robin. Robin used to tease me. I remember her saying a couple of times that all I do is talk about what a great guy Tony is, but I shook it off as just girlfriend talk. No one knows how taken aback I was when I found out that Tony and Robin were together."

"Girl, she's lucky she had you to deal with. I am telling you; I would have kicked her butt all over that school. She wouldn't look at another woman's man again when I was through with her ass."

"What I am curious to know is, how come he is in New York? The last thing I heard they had moved and were living in Georgia. They had relocated soon after they were married."

"Whatever! Just keep me posted on this fiasco."

"I will. We will talk tomorrow."

"OK," Lisa said. "Don't worry about a thing. Like I said, I got your back. Good night. Say hello to James for me."

"Thanks, Lisa. I will tell him. You have a good night too. Talk to you sometime in the morning, OK?"

I hung up the phone. I looked at the clock; it was 7:30 p.m. I realized that James was not in yet and he didn't call. Who knows, maybe he went to the gym.

I walked into the kitchen and started to reheat some of the food I cooked yesterday. I was just taking it out the microwave when I heard the door open, and James walked in.

"Hi."

I responded "Hi" also; no hug or kiss, just walked past me heading to the bedroom.

"I just heated up some dinner. Do you want me to fix you a plate?"

"Not right now. Let me get out of these sweaty clothes. I stopped by the gym to work out. It was a stressful day."

"I know what you mean. Don't forget we have the auditors this week."

"Yeah, I remember you did mention it. How is it going?"

"So far, so good," I replied; I really wasn't about to go into the events of the day. As I sat down to eat, James disappeared into the bathroom, and I ate my dinner alone. I had never told him about the relationship I had with Tony, so I had no intentions of mentioning what transpired today. Right now, I decided I was adopting a wait-and-see attitude; I will deal with it one day at a time.

Tuesday went by quickly. Wednesday morning came, making it three full days that the auditors were here. I had planned to be at work earlier than usual this whole week just to make sure everything was in order, especially for the audit. Ordinarily, I arrive at 8:45 a.m., but this week, I have been out the house so that I could here between 8:15 and 8:30 a.m.

As I got in the elevator, just as the door was about to close, someone stuck his briefcase in the door so that it could reopen. I looked; it was Tony. He stepped in; he looked at me.

"Good morning, Maureen. How are you today?"

"Good morning, Mr. Bradley. I am fine. Thank you for asking."

"No, thank you for speaking to me."

"Why wouldn't I speak to someone who has greeted me?" My mind in the meantime was asking, *what is he getting at? Doesn't he know that I really don't want to talk to him and I really don't care if he speaks to me?*

"You know where I am coming from."

"No, I don't. You greeted me, and I returned the greeting, that's all."

By this time, we had arrived to our floor. As the door opened, I moved quickly and exited. I opened the door to the office and held it open for him to enter. There was this look of rejection on his face, but he kept his composure and walked in without saying another word. I then proceeded to unlock the conference room door so he could get in, and I walked away to my office. We were there at least ten minutes alone before Steven walked in, followed by Mr. King. During that time, he did not come to my office; he stayed in the conference room, I assumed getting his stuff together for the day ahead.

As we settled down and opened for business, Steven buzzed me and asked me to meet him in the conference room. Once inside, Steven said to me that Mr. King was questioning the $5,000 that we spent last November on entertainment.

"Go ahead, Mr. King, ask Ms. Coleman whatever questions you need clarifying," Steve said.

"Yes, Ms. Coleman, I see where $5,000 was spent on entertainment. However, I haven't seen any receipts to say specifically what the money was spent on. Also, the account that is titled 'Fundraising'—where does the funds come from that are being put into that account?"

"I believe there should be receipts in a folder in my office," I responded. "If I may, allow me to give you a brief explanation to your question."

He nodded his head, signaling that it was OK to continue.

"Last year," I began, "we held a reception to help solicit funds for the organization. We wanted to put the word out into the community, and the borough as a whole, about the work we are doing. Donations were collected that evening, and even after the event, there were some donations from individuals. Also, the Munsey Group, for the first-time last year, gave us a donation of $5,000. To be used for publicity purposes. As Mr. White—Steven—can attest, it is our plan over the next five years to have an office in every borough of NYC. The housing problems we face are not generic to Brooklyn only.

As we move forward, our goal is to solicit funds from individuals and to look at ways to raise funds at the grassroots and corporate level."

Mr. King smiled a smile of approval, and he said, "I must commend you both for the excellent job you are doing for the community. Our purpose here is to see that your paper trail for all funds received is well documented because we know if a foundation or the state begins questioning your use of funds, it could get messy. It's our mandate to make sure all your t's are crossed and your i's are dotted. So far, what we have seen is that you are doing just that. Once I am able to review the receipts, we will make sure everything is on the up and up."

"OK. Excuse me while I go find those receipts. Before I go," I asked, "did I explain everything to your satisfaction?"

"Yes, those things I mentioned were our concerns, and you have clarified them for us. All I need now are those receipts."

"Great, let me find them for you."

With that, I left the room, leaving the three men talking. I checked the file cabinet in my office; I know that I had put the receipts and other paperwork associated with the fund-raiser in a drawer. I must confess that I was so busy trying to make sure our first fund-raiser ran smoothly,

I just tucked things away with the intentions of getting back to it later. Obviously, that did not happen; the folder was buried under some files that I had been working on at the time. Maureen, I told myself, this is what happens when you think you are the only one who can handle the fine details. You better learn to delegate more often.

I pulled out the folder, and sure enough, the receipts were there. I collected them and returned to the conference room. Steven had already returned to his office, and the two auditors were discussing something in the file.

"Excuse me, here are the receipts." I handed them to Mr. King.

"Thank you, Ms. Coleman. If we need anything else, we will call."

"OK, sorry about that."

"No problem, Ms. Coleman. It's just an oversight. I am sure everything is in order."

I turned and walked to my office. I hate stuff like that; it makes you look so incompetent.

At the end of the day, Mr. King informed us that most likely, the audit will be completed by the end of the day, Thursday. Inside of me was happy; the past three days had been nerve racking for me. Not so much because of the audit but because of Tony.

I couldn't get over it. After so many years of not seeing him, so many years of trying to get on with my life, he appears and sends my world spinning out of control. I had tried so hard to erase the memory of him and had hoped that by now, I would have been somebody's wife with a family of my own.

On a couple of occasions, as I interacted with Mr. King, I had glanced up to see him studying my face; he quickly looked the other way once he realized I had seen him. There was an unmistakable sadness to his eyes. I knew those eyes so well; they were what attached me to him. In the seven years I had not seen him, he had changed. That boyish look was gone; he had gained weight, he looked like he works out to keep himself fit, his twisted hair was gone—he now wore it low cut—and he had grown a mustache. He also did not wear glasses anymore. I suspect he wore contacts. He had morphed into a handsome man, very professional looking, and he works for a top-level corporation. I guess the past seven years have been good to him. I wondered if he and Robin had any more children.

I didn't want to think of her; even now I could feel some anger begin to rise up. Snap out of it, Maureen.

I brought myself back to the present. I thought of calling Lisa, but there was nothing new to report. I wondered if I should have cut him off as abruptly as I did the other morning in the elevator. I thought I did the right thing; I need to leave that man alone. My poor heart cannot take any more heartaches.

Thursday afternoon, Steven and I sat down with the auditors to go over their findings and recommendations. Surprisingly, Mr. King said that Mr. Bradley would be conducting the review. I sat there; I didn't have much choice but to look at him as he began his review.

"Let me congratulate both of you," he began, "for keeping such excellent records. We especially want to thank Ms. Coleman for her efficiency in supplying us with all requested materials."

I nodded, and I mouthed the words "thank you."

"There was one area of concern that we had," he continued, "and it is regarding the receipts of funds from your fund-raising efforts. We did not see any records of the donors and no copies of the checks that were donated. We noticed that there were three instances where cash was given as donation and no record of who gave it.

Go forward, it is our recommendation that all donations be made by check or money order. A list of donors should be made with the donor's name, address, telephone number, and occupation. You should also make a copy of all checks and money orders received. While I know that you are trying to raise funds and would not like to turn away a donation, no cash donations should be accepted."

"Mr. Bradley," I interjected, "is making copies of donated checks and money orders really necessary? It calls for more filing, and what about donor's banking information?"

He looked directly at me, the muscles in his face softening to a small smile.

"What I would suggest, Ms. Coleman, is that you could scan the check and store them on the computer, password secured. I still believe in backing up file with paper copies, and those can be secured as you secure any of your important documents for the organization. Also, if you ever need to check on any donation, you would have the information on hand, which could save you from having to get the donor to go to his bank for a copy of the check, or whatever the case may be. Does this sound feasible, Ms. Coleman?"

"Yes. Thank you, Mr. Bradley." I managed a slight smile.

The remainder of the review dealt with our funding sources and our tax filings for payroll. With the review completed, Mr. King said that we would receive our formal transcript of the audit within the next two weeks. They both thanked us for making their job easy and wished us continued success with the organization.

We shook hands, and they left. Steven walked them to the door, and I walked to the ladies' room. Once inside, I went into one of the stalls and closed the door, and the tears just rolled down my cheeks. When Anthony walked out the door just now, it was as if I was time-warped to the day when he walked out of my dorm room and said that he had to end our relationship but wouldn't tell me why.

Chapter 4

The audit was over; the office was back to normal. I, on the other hand, was still recovering from seeing Tony again. I console myself that I handled myself very well for the four days he was here. This week was Memorial Day weekend. James and I had plans; we were going to spend the weekend in the Poconos in Pennsylvania. I was so looking forward to getting out of the city and close to nature. I always enjoy our outing; we will drive along the highway, our favorite CDs playing, and we would be talking and laughing and singing along to the music.

As with every trip, I set out a piece of luggage that we would be taking, and I would start packing about three days before it was time to leave. I did this as a way of not forgetting items we may need. I usually pack for James and me. On Wednesday evening, I got in from work, and after I took my shower and had dinner, I started collecting my underwear and sleepwear for the trip. As I was packing, James walked in; he didn't speak. From the look on his face, I could tell he was upset.

"What's the matter?" I asked. He didn't reply.

"James, I am talking to you."

"What? Maureen, leave me alone."

"Come on, James, I haven't done anything to upset you. Why are you taking it out on me?"

"I told you to leave me alone. Can't you just do that?" he replied, his voice harsh.

"You know, this is ridiculous. You walk in, you don't speak to me, and when I ask what's wrong out of concern for you, you want to bite off my head. I think you have a serious problem, my man."

"You know, Maureen, you are the one with the problem. I asked to be left alone, and you still want to create an issue with that. I think it's best if I leave here before I do something I may regret."

He turned around and walked out the door. *What just happened here? I asked myself.*

My excitement for packing went out the door with him. I walked over to sofa. *Lord, I silently prayed, please help me to understand what is happening in my life. Father God, I have tried so hard to do the right thing. I did not let what happened to me with Tony affect the love and care I have for James. I didn't let the actions of one man stop me from giving another man a fair chance at my love. Why is he acting this way?* I ended the prayer.

I thought of calling my mom to complain, but I thought to myself, *I am twenty-eight years old. It's time I stood up and acted like a woman who is in control of her life.*

I sat on the sofa thinking, so many questions drifting through my mind. *What was I doing wrong? Subconsciously, could what happened between Tony and me be affecting my relationship with James?*

Somehow, I didn't think so. It wasn't affecting it in the beginning when we were so in love; I couldn't see why it would be affecting it now. I got up and went to bed. Tomorrow is another day; maybe answers will reveal themselves in the new day, plus I believe that God will show me a way to resolve all this.

Sometime during the night, my eyes opened; I looked first to the cable box to see what time it was. The box said one forty-five. I then turned my head to see if James was there. His spot was empty; he had not returned. *This is new, I thought, he had never done that before.*

I picked up the phone and called his cell; it went to his voice mail. I left a message. "James, please call me. I hope you are all right."

This is such foolish, I told myself. There's no reason for him to act like this. I drifted in and out of sleep until the alarm went off at six forty-five.

As my eyes scanned my room and my attention focused, I could hear someone in the bathroom. I got out of bed and went to the bathroom door. I turned the knob; the door was locked. I checked the kitchen table and his car keys were there, and his shoes were where he always took them off.

I put on the kettle while I waited for him to come out the bathroom. I heard the door open, and he came out and when into the bedroom. I stayed in the kitchen and made myself a cup of tea. I sat at the table and started drinking it. James came out of the bedroom dressed in his shirt and slacks and began to tie his tie. No good morning, no smile.

"James, why didn't you come back home last night? What is happening here?"

"I don't know, and quite frankly I don't care. By the way," he continued, "I have cancelled the trip for this weekend. I need time to sort myself out. I am going to visit my parents this weekend."

"My god, are you serious? I don't believe you. Why are you acting this way?" I said to him. In my mind, I was thinking, *this guy is unreal.*

"Maureen, I just need some time alone right now. I am sorry, but I have to do this."

He turned and walked backed into the bedroom and later reappeared wearing the jacket to the suit. He picked up his briefcase and his keys, and without another word to me, he walked out the door.

I felt the tears start to come to my eyes. I wiped them away quickly. "No, I am not going to cry." He is being so nasty to me for no reason. Maureen, I thought to myself, don't let that man make you cry. You are the one letting him treat you like dirt. You need to get your act together and stand up like the woman you are. He wants to visit his parents—tell the man hasta la vista and get some plans of your own. You have given him too much power over you. If he cared, he would not treat you this way.

I got up from the table and began to get ready for work. *You can handle this,* I confirmed to myself. My mother always says that if we pay attention to that small voice that speaks to us, we will save ourselves a whole lot of grief.

As I traveled to work, the whole scene with James this morning kept replaying in my mind. As I thought about it, I came to the realization that I could pretend all I want and I could try to justify all this and fool myself into thinking that all will be well, but the truth of the matter is, the relationship with James is over. The writing is on the wall as plain as day. What I need to do is to come to terms with this fact and prepare myself so that when it actually happens, I will not go crazy and be heartbroken and bent out of shape.

Later in the day, I called Lisa and told her part of what happened between James and me, and that I will need a plan for the weekend, as I will be alone.

"Listen, Maureen, let's meet after work. There is an after-work spot on Atlantic Avenue. I have been wanting to check it out. Let's go there after work and have a drink."

"Sounds good. I need a couple of drinks for all that I have been going through these past days—Tony and now James. I'll meet you around 5:30 p.m. outside your office."

"OK, I'll see you later."

I barely made it through the day. To everyone, I was the efficient and professional employee; I did not bring my personal problems to work, so I acted like I always do. If only they knew the turmoil and despair I was in at this time.

In my mind, I kept telling myself that I just have to make it through Friday, which couldn't come fast enough for me. I will have the three-day weekend to rest and reset my mind and my life.

As planned, I met up with Lisa, and we walked to the bar and restaurant that had recently opened on Atlantic Avenue. Apparently, it had become a popular hangout for the after-work crowd. The happy hour ran from five to seven, with two-for-one drink specials. We got a small table with two bar stools and ordered a round of drinks—my favorite Aliza and orange juice, and Lisa had Absolute and cranberry.

"What's going on with you and James?" Lisa asked, as she sipped her drink.

"Girl, I wish I knew. He has been acting distant for a while, but I have been taking it in stride, trying to work with it. He came in last night all upset, and when I tried to find out what was wrong, he blew up and walked out. If that wasn't enough, he cancelled our trip to the Poconos."

"Son of a b—tch."

"Lisa!" I practically shouted at her. "Didn't you say that you were going to stop cussing?"

"Yeah, I promised myself I'll stop, but things like what he did gets me upset. You know, relationships are so difficult—you want things to work out, but men come with so much baggage sometimes that you just cannot handle it all. Who the hell knows what is going on in his head? It is as if they expect us to be mind readers.

You see, Maureen, that's one of the reasons I am by myself. I don't have time for men and their childish game. Men have told me that I am dread, but that is not true. There is a lot of love within me that I want to give, but I cannot take it when a man tries to play me for a fool or comes to me with little boy type behavior. I am not having that bullsh-t."

"Lisa, do you think what happened between Tony and me could be having a psychological effect on me, and do you think subconsciously I could be pushing James away?"

"I am no psychiatrist, but I seriously doubt what is happening between you and James is cause by what happened to you and Tony.

Maureen, I know you. You are a sensitive, caring person who gives away all her love and leaves none for herself. All of us have had episodes with men, and I think most of us go into a new relationship with the past relations behind us. Most of us want our relationships to work out so that we could finally be happy and settle down with a responsible, loving man. I know that's what I want.

One thing I will tell you, Maureen," she continued, "stop second-guessing yourself and stop putting yourself down. Look at you—you are beautiful, educated, successful, and independent. Sometimes these things intimidate men. You have to find a man who would be proud to call you his woman because he is strong enough to stand up as your equal and be a man."

"You're right. I have to stop putting myself down and stop acting so desperate."

"Stop settling," Lisa said. "Think carefully about the man you want to live your life with, and that's the man you want to find. Don't look now, but there is a guy at the bar checking you out. Looks like you may have some plans for the weekend after all."

"No, thank you. In my fragile state, I might get carried away and end up in even more problems."

"Flirt, baby, that's the name of the game. When you got it, flaunt it!"

"Lisa, you are crazy. You have put me in my fair share of flirt games in college. I am too old for that now."

"OK, old lady, but if anyone eyes me, hell, I am flirting. After all, I am free, single, and disengaged, and may I say, loving it," she concluded with a laugh.

That was one of the things I like about Lisa; she didn't let anything get her down. She has a free spirit, and she holds nothing back; she calls it like she sees it. Take it or leave it.

We ordered another round of drinks and also ordered from the appetizer menu. We talked, laughed, drank, and ate. Two of Lisa coworkers joined us, and we spent the evening having fun.

I did sneak a peep at the guy at the bar, not bad looking at all—light skinned, nice haircut, slim built, probably about five feet ten. He dressed as if he worked in one of the offices down here. As good as he looked, he really wasn't my type. I like a man that's dark and thick—that is what attracted me to James; he was dark, like rich soil, tall, six feet, broad shoulders, and a cute butt. Yeah, I am leaving that alone, I thought to myself and turned my attention back to Lisa and our friends.

For that period of time, I forgot about James, Tony, and all the things that were cluttering my mind. When I finally checked my watch, it was 9:15 p.m.

"Lisa, it's time we got going. We still have work tomorrow."

"You're right. Let's go."

We said good night to our friends, and Lisa and I left and walked together to the subway station. We got on the first train that arrived, which was the number 3 to New Lots Avenue. This train could take me home, but Lisa would have to change at Franklin Avenue for the number 2. As the train pulled in the Franklin Avenue station, Lisa hugged me.

"Call me as soon as you get in," I told her, I knew that I would get home before her.

"OK, I'll call," she said as she exited the train.

I would get off two stops later at Kingston Avenue. I lived in Crown Heights, and Lisa lived in Flatbush.

I arrived home safely and started to undress. As I about to put my watch and earrings in my jewel box, I noticed a note stuck to the mirror. It was from James. It read: "I am staying at Hal's house tonight. I will leave for New Jersey straight from work tomorrow. James."

Well, if this don't beat all, I thought. I will have to assume that he did not want to talk to me, so the easier thing was to write a note. "It's all right, Mr. James," I said. "You go ahead. The longest day has an end." (Another one of my mother's adages) I crumpled up the note and threw it in the garbage. The phone rang; it was Lisa calling to say she had reached in safely.

"Thanks for a great evening, Lisa. Go get some sleep. We'll talk tomorrow."

"It sure was great. You get some rest also and don't worry about a thing. Talk to you tomorrow, bye."

I hung up the phone. I didn't feel like telling her about the note and that James was staying at his friend's house. I figured it wasn't important.

As I got in bed, I lay there, thinking, so this is what it has come down to. Almost four years of believing that we would get married and settle down is surely walking out the door. Somehow, I wasn't feeling sad about it; I found myself thinking that there is something better in store for me. I actually found myself smiling as a sense of uplift washed over me, and I drifted off to sleep.

Friday morning came, and I went to work as usual. I decided that spending the weekend alone was not a bad idea; this could be a good opportunity to regroup and spend time with myself. It was time that I sat down and seriously think about what I wanted to do with my life and the relationship that I needed to attract. As I thought about it, there was quite a bit I could do to keep myself occupied.

On Saturday afternoon, I decided to give Diane a call. I had spoken to her briefly after her birthday party. I had time on my hands, so I could chitchat. She was happy to hear me, and we talked about her business and a new design she was working on.

"By the way, Diane," I said, there was a woman at your party by the name of Linda. Do you know who she is? I would say she could be about five feet five, dark, slim, very attractive."

"I don't remember inviting anyone by the name of Linda. It's possible she came with one of my guests. Why do you want to know about her?"

I started to tell her that I saw James talking and dancing with her, and when I asked him about her, he became very defensive. I also told her what was happening between us right now.

"Gee, I am sorry to hear all of this. I will check around with a few of my guests who had indicated that they were bringing someone. Maureen, are you prepared to handle it if it comes back that she and James may be involved?"

"To tell you the truth, Diane, I don't know what I am prepared for. So much has been happening that I am feeling a little numb right about now. One thing I know for sure is that it would explain what is happening right now between James and me."

We finished off our conversation with little inquiries about the family, and she promised to get back to me about Linda. As I hung up the phone, I thought of the question Diane asked me: "Are you prepared to handle it if you find out that James is with this woman?" This will be the second time that a man that I loved has left me for another woman. First, Tony left me for Robin, and it's possible that James could be leaving me for Linda. What is it that they see in the other woman that they don't see in me? Why do I keep losing my man to another woman?

Listen, Maureen, my inner voice said, don't go there. You are you, and they are they. There is someone out there who will love you for who you are. Maybe those men did not love you enough.

A little later in the evening, I called my mom; she was at home relaxing. I talked with her for a while. I learned that she and Dad were going out to a brunch on Sunday. I inquired how my brother was doing.

My brother, Charlie, was twenty-five and was still at home. He was working, but I guess not ready to go out on his own. Apparently, my parents didn't have a problem with him being home. I especially knew my mother didn't have a problem; she always says, "When Charlie's ready, he will leave. Until then, he doesn't bother me." I knew my mother loved her boy child. I am sure she loves me too, but I always felt that Charlie had the edge on me.

I didn't mention anything to her about what was going on between James and me. Right now, I wanted to handle things my way. I am sure, at some point, I will get around to telling her.

I spent the rest of the weekend cleaning the apartment, listening to music, catching up on my reading, watching a few of the sitcoms on TV, and walking in the park.

The Park was especially lively over the weekend, as the weather was great, almost like a summer day in July. There were groups of people sitting around listening to music on boom boxes, fellows playing a game of basketball. People outdoor just enjoying the weather and the holiday, Brooklyn style.

As I walked my laps around the track, I could hear the sound of the ice cream truck, which was parked close by the entrance. Its familiar melody beckons children to come for its sweet treats. The short Hispanic lady with her pushcart selling ices was surrounded by a small group of eager children waiting to receive their flavored ices. Favors like coconut, pineapple, and piña colada. I myself enjoy those ices ever so often.

As I walked, I watched mothers with their children running around, playing on the slides and swings, and said to myself, "One of these days, Maureen, one of these days, you will be just like those mothers, playing and watching while their children play. Hold on, girl, its coming."

I found it interesting that I didn't miss James. I wondered how that was possible; if this had happened to me about a year ago, I would have been freaking out. I think, over the past year, the slow disintegrating of the relationship had psychologically been preparing me. I must admit that parts of me felt hurt; I would have so loved for it to have worked out. James and I had a lot in common; we like a lot of the same things, and I felt that those things were good enough to start a life on. Obviously, James had other plans.

Around 7:00 p.m. on Monday, I received a text from James saying that he was still in New Jersey and will be home on Tuesday evening. I read it and I started to dial him, but I could feel the anger start to rise in me. I stopped dialing and put down the phone.

I started talking to myself. "You know," I said, "this is some serious disrespect. He goes away for the weekend, and for him to pick up the phone and call me to at least ask how I am doing, he couldn't do that. Instead, he is texting me like I am nothing to him."

I had to try to calm myself down. I know that there is anger in me that if unleashed, the consequences of it would not be pretty, and then my whole life would be changed forever.

I always try to keep my anger under control; James really had no idea whom he was dealing with. There is a side of me that he has never seen, the side of me what was evil as hell. If only he knew how much he was pissing me off, and I figured, if he wants out, I will let him go and I will not hurt my head about it. He must really see me as a piece of crap that he can do me as he feels like and then walk back in here like nothing happened. I was seething when the phone rang; it was Lisa.

"How are you doing? Did you do anything special this weekend?"

"No, I didn't do anything special." I know my voice was angry.

"Maureen, I know that voice. You're mad as hell right now, aren't you? OK, what happened?"

"It's James texting me, telling me he wouldn't be home until tomorrow evening. Where does he get off at doing this crap to me?" I was practically shouting in Lisa's ear.

"OK, Maureen, calm down, girl. Don't let no man steal your dignity or your peace of mind. He's not worth it."

"But, Lisa, I don't deserve this. I haven't given him cause to treat me this way." I could feel the tears start to come to my eyes. They were angry tears. "He has no right to treat me like this and trample all over my feelings."

"Listen! Girlfriend, like my mother used to say, 'If you can't do with, do without.'"

"What does that mean?" I asked, not really caring. Right about now, I didn't want to hear about those sayings. I was thinking of what James was trying to do to my psyche.

"You know the old people have all these sayings," she replied. "It means if you two cannot get along, get out of the relationship. What sense does it make to stay with someone who is taking you for granted and treating you like dirt? What he is doing is mentally and emotionally abusing you. What is he going to do next? Will he start hitting on you?"

"It will be a cold day in hell if he ever risks something like that. The day he gets so crazy as to hit me, he better leave right away, because if he goes to sleep, it will be all over for him."

"Then I'll have to come and visit you in the big house. Well, before it gets to that, let him go. You didn't go to school, earn your degree, and have a good job to now become an inmate in the prison system. No! My friend, take that out of your mind."

"Whatever." I know that she could hear the disgust and noncaring attitude in my voice.

"Maureen, listen to me. My mom always told us that God doesn't put more on a person than they can bear. I am not a Christian, but my mother would tell us about the Bible daily. She also said that we have to turn to God to help us in our times of trouble and that reading the Psalms was helpful in times of problems. All this anger can do nothing for you right now, and it would only put you in more trouble if you let it fester. You have so much life left to live, girl. Don't throw away your life."

I listened to her. She was right; here I am working myself into a state, and all for what?

"Lisa, thank you. I am so glad you called. You know you are in the wrong field—you should take up counseling."

"Ha," she laughed, "me, counsel? You caught me on a good day. Another day I might have told you to shoot the sucker."

"Girl, you crazy as hell."

"I know, always was. You know I got a touch of the mad blood in me. Get some rest. Tomorrow is another day. You will be all right. Stay strong. Good night. Talk to you tomorrow."

"OK, Lisa. Thanks for everything. Good night."

I hung up the phone. I made myself a cup of tea and tried to calm down. Put on my nightgown and got into the bed.

As I replayed the conservation with Lisa, I recognized that I am the one that's putting myself through all this drama. I have been so wrapped up about getting married and starting a family that I pushed myself to the background for that sake.

Maybe James has recognized the desperation in me about getting married, and he is not really ready. I need to do as Lisa suggested and look to God for help with all these trials. I pulled open the drawer on my nightstand and took out the Bible.

This Bible was given to me by my godmother on my sixteenth birthday, and I have kept it all this time, and have read part of it on several occasions. I had promised myself that I will start reading it but have not made the time to do it.

I started looking for the Psalms and found them. As my eyes scanned the pages, Psalm 27 caught my eyes. It read, "The Lord is my light and my salvation, whom shall I fear, the Lord is the light of my life; of whom shall I be afraid?" I read the entire psalm, and it had such a calming effect on me. I realized that I have forgotten so many of the teachings I knew from going to church when I was younger.

Maybe all of this is showing me that it's time I brought God back into my life. I finished my tea, turned off the lamp, and closed my eyes. "Thank you, Father God. I know that you have my life in your hands, and you have a plan for it."

Chapter 5

"Hi," James said as he walked into the apartment. I was sitting at the kitchen table finishing off my dinner. I started not to answer but decided against it.

"Hi," I responded.

He walked past me and headed for the bedroom. He was in there a few minutes, I assumed changing his clothes. He eventually emerged wearing a pair of shorts and a T-shirt. I thought to myself, *Should I be civil to this man after the stunt he pulled this weekend?*

"Do you want any dinner?" I asked. In my mind I was thinking I really shouldn't care if he wanted something to eat or not. I decided that I am not going to let him change me from the person that I am.

"Sure," he replied. "What did you cook?"

"I made lamb chops and vegetable rice."

I fixed his plate, put it into the microwave to heat, and put some tossed salad in a separate bowl. I placed the salad and his heated food on the place mat, and he pulled out a chair and sat down. "Maureen," he said, "can we talk?"

"Yeah," I replied.

"Listen," he started, "I am sorry about the way I acted last weekend. I had a lot of things on my mind, and I shouldn't have taken it out on you."

I sat there, my face a blank canvas; part of me did not want his apology. If we're married and he had a bad day, would he have done the same thing? What if we had children—was he just going to walk out and leave me alone with them until he cleared his head? No, his behavior was not acceptable.

"Maureen," he said, "are you listening to me?"

"Yes, James, I am listening."

"Well, I wanted to get away because I wanted the time to think. I went about it the wrong way, but I was angry about an incident that happened on the job that day. It got me to thinking, and I realized that I really wanted out. I want out of the job and out of New York. I am thinking of relocating. I feel like I need a new beginning. The other part of this is that I know you have been waiting for me to say I am ready to get married. The truth is that I don't want to get married right now and settle down. I don't think it is fair to you for me to have you hanging and you do not know where I stand."

"James," I interrupted, "what are you saying? Are you breaking up with me?"

"No, I wouldn't say that, but I am letting you know what has been going on in my head."

"You know, James,"—I could feel the flush in my cheeks, a mixture of anger and sadness— "I really thought that you love me and that we had a future together. To come in here tonight after the way, you treated me this weekend and say what you just said takes some nerve on your part."

"Maureen, please listen to me. I don't want to fight. I know what I am saying doesn't sound good, but, Maureen, I am trying to level with you. I cannot keep jerking you around, having you hoping that someday we'll get married and start a family when I am not thinking about that. I am thirty-one years old, and maybe I should settle down and start a family, but, Maureen, I know in my heart that I am not ready to be a husband and a father."

As he spoke, hard as I tried, I could feel the tears start to run down my cheeks. He put down his fork and reached across the table to hold my hand; I pulled it away. I got up from the table and walked into the bedroom and sat on the bed, trying my best to stop the tears. I am not going to let him hurt me anymore, I thought to myself. He followed me into the bedroom and came and sat next to me.

"Maureen, I am sorry. I don't want to hurt you anymore." He reached over and pulled me into his arms; I started to resist but decided against it. He pulled me to his chest, and he kissed my forehead. "I do love you, Maureen, but I don't think I am being fair to you."

"So where do we go from here?" I asked.

"I don't know. I guess we have to work it out. I am leaving it up to you as to what you want to do. If you want me to move out, just give me time to find a place."

"you said you were thinking of relocating. Where are you planning to go, and when?" I asked the question but with mixed feelings. Does it matter to me where he goes? I am not going with him. He has made that clear.

"I am not sure when," he replied, "but my company has offices in Dallas, and I have been looking at some of the vacancies that are available right now, and I plan to apply."

"James, this is hard. I have been doing all that I can, trying to make our relationship work. What happened to all the love that we felt for each other?"

"I don't know, Maureen. Believe me, I never meant for this to end this way. You are right. We started out in love and looking forward to a life together, but somehow along the way, things changed for me. I love you, but I don't want to get married right now. I want to leave New York, but I know that you have all your plans for your organization, and I can't ask you to give up what you are working toward to go with me, and at the end of the day, I still don't want to settle down."

"This hurts, I said, this hurts."

We sat on the bed facing each other with him holding both my hands. I held my head down; I couldn't bear to look in his face. It wasn't because I was ashamed but because I love him, and he wanted to leave. I couldn't bear to look at him; it would only tear me up even more. He let go of my hands and put his hand under my chin, lifting my head up to look at him.

"I am sorry," he said, and his lips gently brushed mine, and he got up and walked out the room.

I got up and went to the bathroom. I washed my face and brushed my teeth. I returned to the bedroom and lay on the bed. My mind was in a whirl. *"So, it's finally here,"* I said to myself. He said he was leaving it up to me as to what I want to do; he knows I have no choice anyway I slice it. He will be leaving; it's just a matter of time.

I guess if he is able to apply and gets the job, he would take it and be gone. How do people deal with heartbreak? This is the second man I have been in love with and the second man who has left me with a broken heart. Tony was the first, and after he betrayed me, I didn't go out with anyone for over two years. I plunged myself into finishing my degree and took men off my mind. Even after that time, I dated two guys but wouldn't let them get close to me. After a couple of dates and no hopes of sex, they eventually stopped calling and asking me out. That was fine with me; I really didn't care.

Tony's leaving had left me bitter, and I wondered if I would ever trust a man again. Over the years, and especially when it first happened, I thought about it constantly, and I still haven't been able to figure how he got hooked up with Robin.

When I first met James, I wasn't all that interested. I met him at a fund-raiser for one of the political groups in Brooklyn.

It was held at a new hotel that was recently opened in downtown Brooklyn. It was a great event, attended by many of the leading and aspiring political folks in Brooklyn. I had attended as a way to network and look for opportunities for my organization. While there, I ran into my friend Louis. I had known him for years from our old neighborhood, and he was very involved. I believe he was a district leader in East New York. While talking to him, he said to me,

"Maureen, I have a nice guy I would like to introduce you to."

"Who told you I am looking for a man?" I replied.

"Well, if you don't want a man, you want a woman instead—I could find you one too."

"Louis," I laughed, "you are out of control. You know I don't want a woman—that's not my thing."

"As they say," he responded, "don't knock it 'til you try it. Seriously, Maureen, I have a nice guy for you to meet."

With that, he grabbed my hand and walked me over to the guy.

"James," Louis said, "this is my friend Maureen. I just told her I have a really nice guy to introduce her to."

"Hello, Maureen," James said, extending his hand to shake mine. "It's nice to meet you. And, yes, if you don't already know, Louis is nuts."

"Trust me," I replied, "I know."

"That being said, let me properly introduce myself. I am James Thomas Jr."

"Nice to meet you, James. I am Maureen Coleman." We both smiled at each other, still holding hands. Louis stood there with this smirk on his face, a smirk that I would have loved to wipe off if I could. For the rest of the evening, we mingled and chatted as best we could in the crowded room with everyone talking. When I was about to leave, he asked me if I had a way home, and I told him I was taking the subway home. He offered to give me a ride home, but I declined. We exchanged business cards and promised to give each other a call. I put the card in my bag, planning to leave it there. About a week later, just as I was getting ready to leave the office, he called.

"Hello, Maureen," he said. "This is James Thomas. We met last week at the fund-raiser."

"Hello, James," I responded. "How are you?"

We made small talk for a minute or two, and then he invited me out to dinner on Friday. At first, I started to hesitate, thinking whether I should accept the invitation, but decided to accept. He worked in Lower Manhattan, and he wanted to know whether I wanted to come to Manhattan to meet him or should he come downtown Brooklyn and meet me. I told him I would prefer to come to Manhattan. He asked me to meet him at West Fourth Street at 6:00 p.m. I agreed, and the conversation ended.

Of course, once I hang up the phone, doubts started to enter my head. *Do I really want to go to dinner with this guy? He seems nice enough, but I am so skeptical of men.* I quieted my mind and decided that a night out might do me some good.

That Friday morning, as I dressed for work, I chose an outfit that could take me from the office to dinner. I wore a dress with a jacket that I could easily take off in the evening, and the dress was perfect for a night on the town.

After work, I took the train to West Fourth and met him by the big McDonalds. As I walked up to him, he smiled and reached over to give me a brief hug. He looked good dressed in his business suit, very corporate looking. He's dark, about six feet, nice body, not too big, just right. He had some hair on this head, but nicely shaped that suited his face, clean shaven.

"Thanks for coming. It's good to see you again," he said.

"Same here," I replied with a smile.

"Let's cross the street. The restaurant is across the street."

We walked to the intersection and crossed over to West Fourth Street. We then walked up to the restaurant. It was a Spanish/Mexican restaurant. We were escorted all the way to the back where there was a garden section. It was lovely, very cozy, with lighted candles and flowers on the tables. The entire section was covered with green plants, which grew around beams and poles. Strings of lights were woven into and through the plants and greenery. The waiter took our order for drinks first, giving us an opportunity to review the dinner menu.

I ordered my usual, and James ordered Red Label and Coke.

"This is nice," I said as a way to break the ice and start conservation.

"I like this restaurant," he replied. "A year ago, a group of us from the office came here for dinner. The food and the service were excellent, and I had said that I would come here again. When I thought of inviting you out, this place came to mind, so here we are."

"OK. Do you have any suggestions for dinner?"

"As I said, the food here is great. If you like avocados, there is an avocado salad that is fantastic. I personally love the braised pork chops with the red wine sauce."

"I think I am in the mood for some seafood. I'll see what the menu has."

I ordered the avocado salad, and it was great as James had said. For the main course, I went with a seafood combination on a bed of saffron rice. It was delicious. We spent ninety minutes eating, talking, and laughing; the time seemed to move so quickly, and before we knew it, our meal was over. As we left the restaurant, he asked if I wanted to take a walk around the village.

Greenwich Village, it has a chemistry all its own. There are so many little shops, bars, cafes, and restaurants along its winding streets. Many of the places are decorated with outdoor lights, and in some doorways, palm readers offer to tell you your fortune.

As it was Friday evening, there were many people around. The start of the weekend usually meant that people go out for dinner and drinks to enjoy the city. As we strolled, we stopped to watch two guys doing an acrobatic dance on the sidewalk. Of course, at the end, they passed the hat around to the crowd who had gathered to watch. We stopped into a small store that carried all types of gemstones, crystals, and beaded jewelry. As usual, my eyes are always looking for unusual things.

It was late September and a really lovely fall evening. It was so easy to get caught up in the moment; we walked and laughed and had fun doing it. At one point, as we were about to cross the street, he held on to my hand. I thought that was so sweet of him. Eventually, we ended up at the parking garage. As we were waiting for his car, I said to him,

"James, thanks for a lovely evening. I can't remember when I last had so much fun."

"You are welcome. I had a wonderful time. Maureen, I hope we can do this again soon."

"Sure," I smiled, "we'll keep in touch."

We drove from the city. I enjoyed the trip home, and the lights of New York City always fascinates me. We came across the Brooklyn Bridge, to Adams Street, and onto Atlantic Avenue. When I arrived at my apartment, he parked the car, got out, and offered to walk me in. I thanked him and assured him that I will be safe. He gave me a quick hug, and I walked into my building.

I don't know if he was hoping I would have invited him in. I wasn't ready for that, and after all, this was the first time I went out with him. I wanted to get to know him a lot better before I thought of inviting him in for a nightcap.

That was the first of many dates, and with each date, I started to like him more and more. I came back to reality as I heard my name being called.

"Maureen," James called to me, "can I get you anything?"

"No," I replied, "I am fine."

"I am going to walk outside for a minute. It's still light out. Do you want to come with me for a walk?"

"No, thanks," I said. "I will be all right."

"OK," he answered back and walked out the room. I heard the apartment door close.

My mind drifted back to James, there was such a magnetic charm about him. He was easy to talk to and there was a fun side of him that always kept me intrigued. After our second date, I found myself looking forward to speaking to him. He has one of the sexiest voices on the phone. We went from calling each other a couple of times a week to every day and sometimes two or three times a day.

The first holiday season after we had begun dating, was wonderful. About a week before Christmas, we had gone out to dinner and then over to Rockefeller Center to see the Christmas tree. We joined the crowd to view the windows at Saks Fifth Avenue and Bloomingdales. As we finished walking around, James walked me over to a horse and carriage, and lifted me in, and we took a ride around Central Park. I had never done anything like that before, and I was thrilled. Before I knew it, I was falling in love with him.

That Christmas, we spent Christmas Eve together. He helped me decorate a small tree that I had bought, and we slept together for the first time. To wake up in his arms that Christmas morning was like a dream and the most enjoyable, loving Christmas gift I ever got. We exchanged gifts; he bought me a diamond tennis bracelet, and I bought him Italian leather gloves and two designer ties.

We spent the day together, and I took him to my parents' home for dinner that evening. Needless to say, my mom had heard so much about him; she was happy to finally meet him. Charmer as he is, he soon became friendly with everyone. My mother and father seem to hit it off with him right away, and he blended right in with his easygoing personality. When we left my parents' home, I felt very elated. I was happy because my parents liked him, and that was a sign for me that this relationship could go places.

Now, four years into it, it has crumbled. *Where did it all go wrong?* I wondered. Soon he will be gone, and I will be all alone and having to start over. I was trying my best to be strong, but what has happened was hurting me to my core.

Maybe my problem is like Lisa said—I give away all my love and leave none for myself. What I have to start doing from now on is to love Maureen too and not put my heart and soul out there to be trampled on, used, and abused.

Chapter 6

Two weeks had gone by since James had his talk with me. We were being polite to each other, just talking on a need-to basis. He was still sleeping in the bed but had not made any attempt to make love to me. To be quite honest, I didn't know if I wanted him to.

For the past two weeks, I have agonized as to how our relationship went from one of possibly marriage and foreverness to one on the verge of separation. *What brings about changes in people?* I wondered. As my mind swung back at forth on the issue, at one point, I thought of trying to influence James to the point of changing his mind; but it dawned on me that I may not be able to convince him, and even if I did, how long would it last, and I still may not get married. I decided I was not going to try. I expected that any day, he will tell me that he applied for a job in Dallas and hopes to interview for it and eventually move.

I myself was thinking of taking a vacation. I had three weeks that was owed to me, and maybe a vacation away from all this would be a good thing at this time. The question of course is, where would I go? The last time I went on vacation, James and I went together. We had decided to take a Disney cruise. We flew to Florida to pick up the ship and spent four days sailing, with stops in the Bahamas and a private island. We came back to Florida and spent three days in Disney World before returning home.

That vacation was fantastic; we were like two kids in a candy shop. Incredibly, this was a childhood dream of both of us to go to Disney World. As we saw parents with their kids, we were saying that as soon as we have our kids and they are old enough to appreciate it, we will be bringing them on a trip like this. That trip was so special to me. I still remember that before we boarded the ship, they offered me a patch for seasickness. I refused; I felt that I didn't need it. That turned out to be a big mistake on my part that night on board the ship as I finished eating my dinner; I had to get up from the table and literally run to the first bathroom I could find. I felt as if my insides were coming through my mouth. I started vomiting; I felt so sick. James took me back to the cabin, and most of the night was spent between the bunk and the bathroom.

By next morning, thank God I was fine. I was able to get up and take an early morning stroll along the deck before having breakfast. I finished the trip with no more mishaps.

We were so in love. We went swimming daily, which had an aphrodisiac effect on James. I also think the two-piece bikinis probably had a lot to do with it too. I had brought a leopard-skin-design two-piece and solid red one. I had to admit they fitted me perfectly. He couldn't keep his eyes off me. The leopard skin suit was held together by two strings around the neck and two strings across my back.

The first time I wore it, as we returned to the cabin, as soon as he closed the door behind him, he reached over and grabbed me.

"Come here, baby," he said. "You know I couldn't keep my eyes off you. You look so damn good, girl."

"Oh, James," I blushed, "cut it out."

Before I could finish my sentence, he had pulled me to him, and his tongue was in my mouth. His kiss fiery, it sent ripples through my body and down to my feet; I could feel my nipples stiffen. His hands reached around my back and untied the strings around my neck, pulling the top down to bare my breasts. It all seemed in one motion, just as quickly his mouth was on my nipples, sucking, his hands holding me tightly around my waist. Before long, he has peeled the bathing suit off me, and his swim truck joined my bikini on the floor.

He resumed kissing me, running his tongue down my chest between my breasts and into my navel. His lips continued traveling all along my belly, kissing and licking as he went. He pulled me over to the sofa, sat down, and pulled me on top of him and slid right into me. A gasp escaped my lips as I could feel the entire length of his manhood reach to the very depth of me.

"Oh, baby," he cried, "do it to me."

I sat on him, his arms around my waist, his face buried between my breasts, kissing them, his hips moving, making every thrust one that sent waves of sensations all over my body. My arms around his neck, my lips kissing his face, his neck, and his shoulders.

"Oh god, baby, Maureen, I love this so much," his speech barely audible and filled with all the emotions that engulf his mind at this moment, his hand holding on to my thigh, as he assisted in my up-and-down movement on him. I could feel my body responding to him, a bolt of pure electricity that shot through me and wrapped in its clutches. I heard myself saying, "James, James, baby," and for that moment, my body trembled with pure delight. He was right behind, the strength of arms around me as he released all the passion and himself into me, and then his arms fell away from my waist. For a few minutes, we didn't move, our body spent from the intensity of the moment.

"Girl, you are going to kill me. You are too damn sweet. I love you, baby."

"You are crazy. It's more like you are going to kill me the way you throw him around." I lifted myself off of him and reached out and touched his now-limp manhood.

"You have to remember you are not small."

"What? This little thing?" He held it in his hand with a laugh.

"Yeah, right, trust me, he's not little when he gets hard," I replied.

"But you love it, don't you?" he said with this smug look on his face.

"Whatever," I said with a big grin.

I headed to the bathroom; he followed, tapping me on my behind as I turned to walk away.

That was the vacation of a lifetime; we were so in love. For us, every day was sunshine; we enjoyed each other's company, and we just had fun. By the time I returned from that vacation, I was so deeply in love with James. I was at the point where I was ready to settle down to be his wife and the mother of his children; all I needed was for him to propose to me, and we were going to be married in nothing flat. Now that was not going to be instead of our love growing, it has slowly eroded away.

Part of me wanted to get away, but another part of me wanted to stay. I knew that if I went away, I would still be worrying and thinking about this whole situation. To go away by myself and be alone, that would be no good, as I would have more time to dwell on the negative of all this. I figured that if I stayed, at least I would be able to throw myself into the job and look for things to do to keep my mind off this.

Of course, the most important lesson to be learned from all this is that you cannot run away from your problems. You have to be willing to confront them and deal with them no matter how painful they may be. As I weighed everything, I concluded that going on vacation was not the best thing for me to do at this time.

On Tuesday evening, as I came in from work, James came in right behind me. I took off my shoes and sat at the kitchen table for a minute. I heard the apartment door unlock, and James walked in. As he walked past me, he reached over and touched my hair.

"Hi, are you OK?" he said.

"Yeah, I am good."

He walked away, going into the bedroom. He emerged a few minutes later wearing a T-shirt and his briefs. He went into the fridge and took out a can of soda, pouring half of it into a glass, and began drinking it.

"Maureen, I am leaving for Dallas on Thursday afternoon."

"Oh, you got an interview?"

"Yes, I have an interview at ten o'clock, Friday morning."

"Good for you. Good luck. I hope everything works out for you."

"Maureen!"

He came behind the chair and put his arms around my neck; he bent over and kissed the nape of my neck.

"I hope everything does work out. I really want this job."

I got up from the chair as a way of getting his hands from around my neck. As I stood up, he pulled me to him and held me tightly.

"Don't, James, I can't do this."

"Maureen, this is not easy for me either. I know that I have hurt you badly, and believe it or not, I don't want to leave with you hating me for this."

"James, I don't hate you. I am hurt, but I don't hate you. I don't know when we grew apart, but as for me, I loved you and I wanted to be your wife. I will get over it. I truly do wish you the best and hope you get the job you want."

"Maureen, I don't know if you would believe me. I did love you, and in a way, I still do, but there is a restlessness in me that I am not satisfied with the job I currently have and the life I live. I want more than what I have right now. I feel like I am doing the right thing by not holding on to you and involving you as I chase my destiny."

"Right now, it's difficult for me to see it from your point of view, but I am trying. I understand, and I will get over it."

I extricated myself from his arms, and he let me go reluctantly. I walked into the bedroom. He didn't follow, and I was glad for that. I didn't want him hugging me because deep within, if he tried to make love to me, I would probably do it; but I know that afterward, I would hate myself for being too weak. I would feel used, and that is not how I wanted to feel, so the best thing to do was not to even entertain the thought.

So, he's off to Dallas, my mind couldn't stop thinking. If he gets the job, it would only be a matter of weeks, or maybe less before he moves on with his life.

I guess when he gets back, and he has to relocate; we would discuss what will be done with his furniture that he had integrated into the apartment when he moved in. I am sure he would not ship anything; I didn't think it would be worth it. Mostly likely, it would be cheaper for him to buy stuff there and set up his apartment once he finds one.

If he doesn't get the job, we will still have to discuss his moving out, as I did not want to continue sharing living space with him. As it is, sleeping in the same bed with him has an uncomfortable feel to it. We both have been staying on our side, staying cautious not to invade the other person's space. This is what it has come to, from being wrapped up tight together to now each of us having our side of the bed.

The remainder of the evening, he spent on the computer, getting stuff together, and I watched as he walked around packing and deciding what to carry. He did ask my opinion on the suit to wear for the interview, and I suggested that he go with the dark gray instead of the blue. I really didn't think he needed my opinion, as he does a beautiful job of being coordinated and in style. I think it was his way to try to break up some of the heaviness that seems to fill in all the spaces around us. It felt as if we were in this uneasy setting of walking tiptoed around each other, trying to be cordial while all along we are both feeling the effect of the tearing apart of our relationship. Well, it's almost over, and come what may, I will go on.

Chapter 7

The doorbell rang. I walked to the door and opened it; it was Lisa. I had invited her over to hang out with me for the afternoon. James had moved out last weekend, and for the past week, I had not tried to put the apartment in order; it was not that it was messy, but with James leaving, it felt as if it had this emptiness. He had packed all his clothes and personal items and rented a van to take the stuff to New Jersey. He had interviewed for the job in Dallas and got it, so he moved on with his plans of relocating. Once he got back from Dallas that Sunday, by the Tuesday, they had called to tell him the job was his. He had a week to get things in order, and he started arranging his business immediately. I was happy for him, and secretly, I was hoping that he might have held out some shred of hope by saying that I could come and visit to see if I like the place. Nothing of the sort was done. We discussed what pieces of furniture I was keeping and what he was going to store at his parents' home in Camden, New Jersey. Once everything was in place, he politely hugged me good-bye, and he was on his way. In the back of my mind, I wondered what could have brought on such a change in him that he was willing to pull up stakes and relocate all the way to Texas. Clearly, it was not just about leaving me; he wanted a new beginning somewhere else far away.

I am not going to pretend that this was not heartbreaking for me. After four years and what we had, I hurt like hell, but you cannot make a person want you. I felt that I could as well get over it, as no amount of crying and feeling sorry for me was going to change the situation.

"So, he's gone," Lisa said. "Ah well, you know, Maureen, you may think that this is hard now, but, girl, a whole new life may be opening for you."

I shook my head. "Right about now, all I am trying to do is take this one day at a time. My first priority is to clean up this place and try to put it back to the way I had it when I lived here by myself."

"You know what you need to do—" Lisa said, "look for a new apartment. I think you need to get out of this place. A new apartment will bring you a new outlook on life. Maureen, are you listening to me?"

Lisa reached over and touched my arm. For a minute there, my thoughts had taken me away from the room.

"I am sorry, Lisa. I heard you, and my mind started thinking about where I would want to live."

"Why don't you look in Bed-Stuy? If you find something close to the A train or C train, all the better for you—it would put you closer to your job."

"Yeah, that's true, but I am not sure about Bed-Stuy. It doesn't have the greatest reputation. There is always something happening over there."

"I personally think it's the same all over. I don't think they say anything positive about my neighborhood either. I am sure people say that Flatbush is not safe, but I love my neighborhood, and I have never encountered any problems in all the time I have been there. Anyhow, think about what I am telling you. Changing your apartment may bring about a change in your life that will be for the better."

"I hope you're right. I need a complete makeover. I have to put the past behind me and try to move forward. James certainly has done it, and I don't think he worried about it—he just made up his mind and moved on."

"I hear that," Lisa replied. "You know men are different animals than us. Our problem is we let our hearts rule us. We get all emotional and mushy when we are in love. Men, on the other hand, let their head and their genitals rule them, so they don't get all sentimental about a whole lot of stuff. That is why I think it is easier for them to move on."

Lisa always seems to make sense in the things that she says. Maybe I should think of moving and starting out fresh in a new location.

"You know, Lisa, I think I will do it. I will start looking at listings in the papers tomorrow."

"Papers? Have you forgotten what year it is? Girl, you better get online and do your research. These days, you can take a virtual tour of apartments so you see the place, which will give you an opportunity to see if it worth taking a trip to look at it. It will save you and the real estate agent a lot of grief by not looking at apartments you may not be interested in."

"Girl, you have to forgive me. Right now, my head is still in a fog, still not thinking clearly."

"Snap out of it. Maureen, I know that things may seem rough right now, but you are a strong woman—you will make it. One of these days, James is going to come to a realization that he let a beautiful and loving woman slip through his fingers. But if I were you, I wouldn't worry about a thing. Before long, some man is going to come along and snap you up. Just remember to check if he has a brother for me."

"Crazy woman," I said, looking at her with a smirk on my face, "why don't you find a man and see if he has a brother for me? You may do a better job of picking the right man for me."

"Yeah, sure, but don't wait on me. I have been looking, and I cannot find anything that suits me, so the search continues."

We finished off the visit talking and rearranging furniture. After she left, as I thought of what she said, I began to like the idea more and more of finding a new apartment. This apartment was nice, and I had liked it from the first time I saw it, but now, as nice as it was, the memory of James lingers, and I found myself missing him and feeling lonely when I come home in the evenings. When I lived here alone, I never had that feeling, but James has left his mark on the apartment and on me.

I can't do anything about the memories; time will eventually take care of those, but I certainly could do something right now about where I live.

Over the next week, I took Lisa's advice and contacted a real estate agent; actually, it was the same company I had used when I got my current apartment. Last time, I had dealt with a very pleasant and professional man by the name of Johnny; but this time, I met a woman by the name of Liz. She seemed very knowledgeable and was very excited about showing me some places. She was also willing to work around my schedule, and if weekends were better for me, that wouldn't be a problem.

After speaking with her and listening to the location of two apartments in Bed-Stuy, I decided to set up an appointment to meet with her this coming Saturday. On Saturday, I got dressed; it was hot outside, and I decided to wear a floral strap sundress sun. I pulled my hair into a ponytail, grabbed my bag and my sunglasses, and went out the door. I drove to the address of the first listing where I was supposed to meet Liz. The address was on Hancock Street between Kingston and Nostrand Avenue. I met Liz in front of the house. It was a brownstone. It has long steps up to the front door. We rang the doorbell, and a middle-aged man appeared at the door.

"Mr. Hinds,"—Liz extended her hand— "good morning. How are you today?"

"Good morning to you, Ms. Perry. I am well, thank you."

"This is Ms. Coleman, the lady that is interested in the apartment."

I shook his hand. He then proceeded to lead us up the stairs toward the apartment. We climbed two flights of stairs to the top apartment. It was a one-bedroom with a spacious living room, dining room/kitchen, and the bathroom. It was not bad, but it did not tickle my fantasy. Walking up and down two flights of stairs daily or every time I had to go outside did not inspire me either. I looked it over one last time and told Liz that I'd like to think about it some more.

Mr. Perry kept telling me that the neighborhood was great and that he has owned the house for the past fifteen years. He said that everyone on the block looks out for each other and that it's a safe area. I listened, I smiled, and I thanked him.

We left and went to the second location, which was located on Sumpter Street between Saratoga and Thomas Boyland Avenue. This was a newer house, and the apartment was located on the first floor. Again, it was nice, but I didn't get that thrilling feeling as I looked it over.

As we left the house, I stopped to talk to Liz. I told her that I wanted to continue looking. I told her that if any new listings came in that she should call me, and I could be willing to look at apartments in the evenings after work. She agreed, and we said our goodbyes. We both drove off, going in separated directions.

As I drove along, I noticed a park, and I decided to stop for a minute. It was about 11:30 a.m. There were young men playing basketball, and I could see parents with their kids on the swings and the slides. I parked the car, locked it, and walked into the park. As I walked along, a ball came rolling, stopping just inches away from my feet. I figured it belonged to one of the children. I bent down to retrieve it just as a man ran up to me and said,

"Sorry, miss, my son is going to be a great pitcher somed—" He didn't finish the sentence, and I understood why when I straightened myself up and looked into his face. It was Tony. We stood there for a minute staring at each other.

"Oh," he said, "hello, Maureen."

I felt tongue-tied. *How is this possible?* I asked myself silently.

"Hi," I replied. I know my face registered pure surprise; never in my wildest dreams would I have imagined that I would run into Tony here in this park. What trick of fate could have made me stop there at this time that I would see this man? As I stood there pondering all this, a little fellow between the age of six or seven ran up to Tony.

"Dad, come on, throw me the ball."

"Hold on. Come, I want you to meet someone." He finished walking up to us and reached into his father's hand to take the ball.

"Ezra, I want you to say hello to Miss Maureen."

"Hello, Miss Maureen," and with that, he threw his little arms around my legs. I was caught off guard; I just stood here, unsure of what to do next. His father must have seen the surprised look on my face, and he reached over and pulled him away.

"Sorry about that. He wants to hug every woman he meets. I think he misses his mother. Here, Ezra, go throw the ball. I will be right there."

When my mouth finally opened, I said, "His name is Ezra. You named him after my father?"

"Yes."

"Why?" I couldn't believe his answer.

"Didn't you say that when we had a son, you wanted to name him after your father?"

"Yes, I remember us having a discussion about children, but I still don't understand why you would name your son after my father."

"Because, Maureen, he should have been our son."

"Oh!" That's all I could say.

Once my brain digested that answer, I wanted to know why he said that Ezra misses his mother.

"You said he misses his mother—where is Robin?"

He looked at me. He lowered his eyes to the ground, shook his head, and looking again at me, said, "She died."

It took a minute for my brain to process the words he had said. I heard myself asking, "Robin died? When?"

"Yes, she passed about two years ago."

In an instant, so many things came flooding through my mind. Robin dead? What could have happened? She used to be my friend before she did what she did to me. We were about the same age—how could she just die like that? "I am sorry to hear that."

"Thank you."

For the first time since we stood there, I looked him fully in the face, into his eyes, the eyes that at this moment had lost the sparkle they once had. It was as if the light in them had been dimmed.

"Maureen, is there any way possible we could meet and talk? There is something that I need to tell you."

I was still reeling from the news of Robin's death. "Sure," I heard myself say, "call me."

"Wait a minute, let me key your number into my phone—that way, I know I will have it."

I gave him the number. "Is it OK if I call you later this evening?"

"Sure, you can call me."

We stood there looking at each other, almost in a trancelike setting, as Ezra walked up to his father, pulling on his hand and breaking the connection.

"Come on, Daddy, come and throw me the ball."

"OK," he said, "I am coming. I'll call you later, Maureen. Thanks."

As he turned to walk away, I did the same thing, heading back to my car.

Once inside, I sat behind the wheel and replayed the whole conservation I just had with Tony. *Robin dead?* Unbelievable! I wondered what he wanted to talk to me about. I had been right about the sadness I saw in his eyes when he was at my office during the audit. Robin had died, leaving him to raise this kid.   Suddenly, my problems seemed small next to what he has gone through and, I am sure, still going through.

Another thing that puzzled me was when he said that he named the boy Ezra because he should have been our son. I started the car, and I headed for home. I wanted to get home to process this incident.

Once inside the apartment, I thought of calling Lisa to tell her about it but decided not to. The remainder of the day went by as if I was in a daze. I kept reliving the whole incident that took place in the park.

I felt sad for Tony and little Ezra; I even felt sad about Robin. Yes, her actions had seriously impacted my life, but through it all, I never wished bad for her or tried to seek any kind of revenge against her and Tony, and now to hear that she died, it was news that I never expected to hear.

When Tony was in the office for the audit, I assumed that they had moved back to New York from Georgia—that was why Tony was working for Miller, Green, and Cohen, whose offices were in Manhattan. As I thought about it, him having to raise this child on his own, it made sense for him to come back to New York, as most likely, his parents and most of his family still lived in Brooklyn. Chances are he needed all the help he could get as a single dad.

When I thought of how little Ezra threw his arms around me, my heart just melted. I have such a love of children and want so much to have a child of my own; I thought he was just the most adorable little boy I have met in a long time. For those few minutes we stood there talking, I could see that little Ezra looks a lot like his father. His skin color looks more like Robin's, who was light complexioned.

In my mind, I could see Robin now. She was tall, about five feet seven, slim, and she had a soft naturally curly type of hair. She wore her hair short. Looking at her, you could see that she was mixed race. I remember us talking one time about our family, and I told her that my great-grandparents came from the West Indies. She said that her family was mix with white, Native American Indian, and black. Come to think of it, I never did ask her how she ended up in college upstate New York, as she said most of her family lived in Georgia. She was a beautiful girl, and we used to have fun when we all hung out together; I never knew that behind my back, she had designs on my man, and she took him. I wondered how long Tony could have been sneaking out and seeing her.

Now he wants to talk to me. All these years, I never heard from him, until he shows up at my office to do the audit. Now today, of all the parks in Brooklyn, I had to stop in that park. I really don't know what to make of all of this; it's as if it's some unimaginable coincidence.

Just after 6:00 p.m., Tony called. "Hello, Maureen, I still haven't gotten over meeting you today. I think it's nothing short of a miracle that we were able to meet."

"I know what you mean. I can't believe it myself. By the way," I continued, "I am curious to know what Robin died of?"

"She developed breast cancer about six months after she had Ezra. It went into remission and stayed away for almost three years. It surfaced again, and this time, she lost the fight. Maureen," he continued, "before she died, she made me promise her that I would tell you that she said that she was sorry for what she did and please forgive her."

"Oh,"—I let out a sigh— "I don't know what to say."

"Maureen, I would like very much to sit down with you so I could explain some things to you. I think when you hear what I have to say, you will understand why Robin wants your forgiveness. There is more to this than the obvious."

"Tony, this is so sudden and unexpected. I have to think about it. Is it OK to call you back on this number that appears on my phone?"

"Yes, of course."

"All right, I will save it in my contacts. I will give you a call during the week and see if we can arrange an evening to meet. Is that, OK?"

"Yes, that's fine. Thanks, Maureen. I will listen for your call. Good night."

"Good night and say good night to Ezra for me also."

I could hear the smile in his voice as he said, "Will do. Thanks."

I hung up the phone and sat on my sofa, a thousand thoughts going through my mind at lightning speed. Robin wants my forgiveness, but as he said, not for the obvious, which would be that she stole my man. So, there is more to this story? I questioned myself. Then the next question is, do I really want to meet Tony to talk? I have to take my time and think this through. Suddenly, everything is coming at me fast and furious.

Right now, the best thing for me to do is to get some rest and clear my mind.

Chapter 8

"So Robin died—I cannot believe it," Lisa said as we sat having some buffalo wings with blue cheese dressing.

A week had gone by since I accidentally ran into Tony in the park. I had promised to call him so we could talk, but I was undecided as to whether I wanted to sit down with him or not. As Lisa sat across the table from me in my apartment, I was still coming to terms with the news I had heard a week ago.

"I wonder what he could have to tell you." Lisa continued, "Maureen, this is a tough one. I am sure Robin felt guilty as hell for what she did, so she decided to confess her sins before she died. Lucky for her, God is a forgiving God, but do you feel you can forgive her, Maureen?"

"Lisa, I don't know, I am praying on it."

"What has my curiosity piqued is that he said she wants your forgiveness, but not for the obvious," Lisa said. "What do you think he meant by that?"

"I thought of that also," I said.

"The obvious is that she broke up you and your boyfriend, but he is implying that there is more to it than that.

"You know," Lisa continued, "life is so fleeting. Who would have thought that Robin will develop breast cancer and be dead by twenty-six? Maureen, I cannot tell you what to do, but meet with him and hear what he has to say. It is as if they both have been punished for what they did. Who knows, he too may want your forgiveness. Sometimes guilt weighs on people's minds and affects them in a lot of ways. I am sure he also feels some guilt and is reaching out, hoping you will ease his conscience."

"Lisa," I said, "I will think about it. I know you always give me good advice, so I will let you know if I decide to do it."

"OK," she said. "Don't wait too long. You know inquiring minds want to know." She laughed.

"Crazy woman, maybe I should have him meet with the both of us, and I will tell him you are my shrink."

"Girl, that sounds good. I would act that part really well. I will get me a gray pantsuit and a pair of glasses to give me that intelligent serious look, and I will be 'Dr. Lisa Williams, psychiatrist.'"

"That's all right," I said. "I will handle this myself."

"I know that right." She laughed.

After Lisa left, I thought of calling Tony, but I kept putting it off.

You really should call him, something inside me said. I picked up the phone, and then I put it back down. As I laid it on the table, it rang.

"Hello, Maureen," the voice said; it was Tony. "Did I get you at a bad time?" he asked.

"No," I replied. "Funny, I just picked up the phone to call you, and I put it back down."

"I was listening for your call during the week, and as I did not hear from you, I thought I would give you a call. I hope you don't mind."

"Not at all. I thought of calling several times this week but kept putting it off."

"I was wondering," he said, "do you think we could meet tomorrow afternoon about four o'clock? We could sit on the porch, and I will make a pitcher of lemonade, and we could talk."

To lighten the tension I felt, I jokingly said, "Shall I wear a broad-rim hat? It sounds very southern to me, sitting on the porch, drinking lemonade on a hot summer afternoon." We both started laughing. That was one of Tony's traits—he had a healthy sense of humor.

"I would be honored by your presence, broad-rim hat not mandatory," he replied between chuckles.

"OK, I'll see you at 4:00 p.m. What is the address?"

"It's 479 Bainbridge Street between Howard Avenue and Saratoga. Call me when you are outside, and I will come out to meet you."

"All right, I'll see you tomorrow. Good night." I hung up the phone.

I poured myself a glass of juice, and I sat on the sofa. I thought to myself, *I am not sure he could tell me anything I wanted to hear,* but I was intrigued.

Robin wanted my forgiveness, and I have been praying on it. I don't know if I will be able to forgive her for what she did; she took the first man I ever loved from me. I wondered if she could have had any idea of how much pain she made me suffer.

I was in love with Tony, and I knew, or at least I believed, he was in love with me, and then she comes along and destroys everything. Yes, we talked girl talk, but she could have never known how deeply I felt about Tony. I would see him, and my heart would somersault. I couldn't think of him without that warm fuzzy feeling of wanting him, to hug and kiss him. Another thing she couldn't have known is that he was the first man to make love to me.

You know what's so funny is that I never had a talk with my mother or father for that matter about saving myself for my husband. I guess standards have changed so much in the world that no one expects you to be a virgin on your wedding night. I had not even thought of it, but while some of my friends lost their virginity in high school, I went off to college still intact. I had not met any boy that I felt that great about.

I was always a bookworm, and I am sure some of my friends thought me a nerd, but sex at that time did not interest me. As I sat there, it all unfolded before me. I remembered it so well as if it had happened yesterday.

After that day we had the coffee together, we started meeting for lunch or an afternoon snack between classes. The more I saw him, the more I liked him. About two months after we met, it was a snowy day in March, and as we walked along on our way to the dorm, I felt myself slipping, and I just knew I was going to hit the ground. Tony reached over and grabbed me, holding on to me tightly and pulling me to him.

"Oh my god," I shouted, as his arms went around me, "thank you for saving me." For a few minutes, he held me close, and as I raised my head to look him in the face, his face slowly met mine, and his lips touched mine, gently at first, and as my lips parted, his tongue entered my mouth, and he kissed me so deeply. When he released me, we both looked at each other and started giggling simultaneously. That was our first kiss.

Two weeks later, the first weekend in April was his birthday. We had discussed what we wanted to do for his birthday, and we decided to rent a cabin in the Catskills and spend the weekend. That Friday, after our only class, we set out. It was a two-and-half-hour trip, but we listened to music and chatted as we drove. When we arrived and checked in, we went over to our cabin.

The area was beautiful, trees and shrubs. As it was early spring, the flowers were just beginning to grow in. The cabin was lovely. It had a small kitchen, a bathroom, a large room with a fireplace, and a bedroom area. It was just the right size for us for an intimate getaway. On the table by the sofa was a lovely bouquet of mixed flowers in a vase. As we set down our luggage, Tony looked at me and said,

"Those flowers are for you."

"What?" I know I sounded surprised. "I thought they were part of the décor. It's your birthday, not mine."

"Yes, I know, but they are for a woman who is so special to me."

"Oh, Tony," I said while smiling and blushing from ear to ear. He walked up to me and hugged and kissed me. I went over to the vase, and the card attached read, "To Maureen, Love Tony." We went to dinner, and I presented him with his birthday present, a watch. It was not an expensive watch, but sporty, the kind you could wear every day and be fashionable.

It was a lovely evening; we ate our dinner, talked, laughed, gazed into each other's eyes, and fed each other some of our dessert. I am sure anyone seeing us knew that we were in love; we just had that glazed look on us.

When we finally returned to the cabin, someone had lit the fireplace, and the room was cozy and warm. At that point, Tony went into the kitchen and came back with two champagne glasses and a bottle of champagne. He popped the cork while I held the glasses and he poured. We lifted our glasses to a toast, with me saying,

"Happy birthday, babe. I wish you many more."

He replied, "Thank you." We touched our glasses and drank. I had to admit, I had no experience with alcohol. This was the second time in my life that I tasted champagne. The first time was at my cousin's wedding about two years ago. I took a sip, and I thought that it was not all that it was cracked up to be.

Tonight, however, it tasted great, and before long, I had finished my glass and started on a second glass. We sat on the sofa facing the fire, kissing each other between sips.

"Maureen," Tony said, "you have made this birthday the best I ever had."

"Oh, I'm sure you must have had some other nice ones before," I replied.

"If I recall correctly," he continued, "I have had three birthday parties. One when I was six, the next was for my sixteenth birthday, my parents took me and a couple of my friends to see the Knicks play at Madison Square Garden. For my twenty-first birthday, last year, the family kept a lunch after service.

By the way, do you know that my father is a pastor?"

"No, I didn't know that."

"Well, yes, I am just like that song by Dusty Springfield—I am a son of a preacher man."

We both burst out laughing. "You are something else," I said to him between the laughter.

"All my birthdays were good, but none of them can compare to this, and it's all because you are here with me, share this evening with me. You make my life special. I have never been in love before. I never thought of looking for a girlfriend. To hear my father tell it, he said, "Everything has its place. First, you get an education. Then you think about finding a nice girl to settle down with." I think I have done it; I am almost finished. In the next couple of months, I graduate, and I have found my girl. I love you. Maureen."

He ran his hand along my cheek and smoothed my hair away from my face. His hand reached to the back of my dress and slowly started to pull the zipper down. As he got halfway down, I stood up, and he pulled it all the way down. I allowed the dress to fall to the floor, and I stepped out of it, picked it up, and put it across the chair. Tony got up and proceeded to pull his sweater over his head and took his pants off. His arms went around my waist; our bodies touching skin to skin. He continued kissing my shoulders and my neck. He reached behind my back and unhooked my bra.

"This is beautiful," he said as he held the bra in his hand, "but nothing to compare to what they held."

He leaned over, running his tongue all along my chest until he reached my breasts, his lips kissing them. He straightened himself up, and taking my hand, we walked over to the bed. His arms around my waist and pulling me to him, we fell backward onto the bed, thereby putting me on top of him. His hands cupped my face, smoothing the hair away from my face. He turned me over, and his lips traced a line all along my rib cage onto my belly and down along my leg. He reached up with both hands and pulled my panties down and off completely. His tongue played with my navel and along the bikini line of my belly.

As he tried to enter me, he met with resistance. He tried again, and I know I flinched. Looking at me, he whispered, "Are you a virgin?"

I meekly answered, "Yes."

A sigh escaped his lips. "I am sorry, I didn't know."

"Please don't stop, I want to do this."

"Are you sure, Maureen?"

"I am sure," I said.

He kissed me, and then he said, "Can I tell you something?"

"What?" I said.

"I have never done this before either," he admitted, his eyes still fixed on my face.

"Really?" I was shocked. "So, this is a first for both of us?"

"Yeah," he whispered.

I wrapped my arms around his neck and gave in to the experience of first love. Together, we both experienced what is meant to make love and be in love. The fireplace aglow with the crackling fire was nothing to compare to the heights of desire and passion that engulfed us. Two people who gave themselves to each other unconditionally. Touching, sighing, inhaling each other's breath; it was something I will never forget. We lay wrapped in each other's arms until sleep claimed us. Lying there together, it was as if we were all alone in the vast expanse of the universe. The stars and moon rotated around us as we floated and drifted in a sea of bliss.

When I opened my eyes that morning and saw my beloved still sleeping, in the faint light of the room as morning began to dawn, I knew I had given myself to the right man, and I prayed that he also felt that he had given himself to the woman he wanted to share his life with. I looked at his face without his glasses, so beautiful, his form so lovely silhouetted by the little light that filtered into the room. All my emotions flooded through me; I love him so much. He had done to me what no one else had ever done, and for that, my love for him was assured.

We spent the Saturday on a nature hike and went swimming in the indoor pool. Of course, we couldn't keep our hands off each other, touching, hugging, and kissing. By the time we left on Sunday afternoon, we had learned so much about each other, and we both talked about what we would like our future to be. As we talked, I told him that I was surprised to know that at twenty-two, he had never slept with anyone. He said that his father counseled him and his two sisters about sex. He urged them not to fall prey to the desires of the flesh but to keep themselves whole until they found the man or woman they wanted to marry. He said his father told him that what he asked of his daughters, he also asked of his son. He said his father had raised them strictly believing that the behavior of his family should be an example for his congregation. I got the sense that he listens and does as his father instructed, and I didn't believe that he would want to disappoint his father in anything he did. Listening to him, I wondered if by him sleeping with me that he felt so strongly about me that he went against his father's wishes and had premarital sex. I found all this so interesting that, in 2001, there were still families out there that had that type of family structure.

As I sat there thinking all of this over, I wondered how a man who waited all that time before he could sleep with someone, who had been brought up with a sense of honor and responsibility, ended up cheating on me with Robin. It was so out of character for him, but he must have done it; how else did Robin become pregnant and he had to marry her? And if he did it, why does he feel he owes me an explanation? He didn't explain it when he broke up with me, how after all this time he wants to set the record straight. Should I really go tomorrow and listen to him? the question sounded loudly in my brain.

"OK, enough, Maureen. Go get some rest. See how you feel in the morning," I said to myself loudly as I got up from the sofa. I walked to the kitchen sink, washed the glass, and went off to bed.

Chapter 9

"Have a seat," Tony said.

I sat in the chair as he indicated.

"This is different," I said. "I expected your porch to be at the front of the house."

"I know that's usually how they are in the city. That is one of the reasons I bought this house. This was the only house I saw with this setting. I like the idea of sitting out here at the end of the day and just retreating from the rest of the world," he answered.

The porch was an enclosed area of the house just off the kitchen. It had three large windows that looked out onto the backyard. There were two armchairs and a chaise, a round glass table with a pitcher of what I assume to be the lemonade he said we could have, and two glasses.

"Different, but very nice," I said.

"Thank you. I am glad you could make it. Would you like a tour of the house, or we could do it later?" he asked, still standing looking at me.

"Let's do it later," I said, having settled into my chair.

"As promised, I made my signature lemonade, hope you like it." With that, he retreated to the kitchen and came back with an ice bucket. He proceeded to place a couple of ice cubes in the glasses and poured the lemonade.

"Cheers," he said, "and welcome."

"Cheers," I replied, "and thank you." I tasted the lemonade; it was good. "Is this a secret recipe?"

"You could say so. I used a dash of essence I discovered by accident."

"It's safe to drink, right?" I asked, the glass still to my lips.

"Define safe," he responded with a big chuckle. "Don't be silly. It's mixed essence, the real good one, the one from the islands."

I started laughing also; this was Tony, the eternal prankster with a healthy dose of humor.

"I see you haven't lost your weird sense of humor," I managed to say between the laughter.

"It's what keeps me going." His facial expression changed from that of smiling to taking on a more serious look.

"Maureen, I asked you here because there is something I have to tell you, and now that you are here, I feel as if I don't know where to begin. You know, I have prayed for an opportunity like this, and I have thought about it for so long, and now that it's finally here, you are finally here, I feel tongue-tied and nervous as hell."

"Tony," I said, "you know what they say, just start at the beginning."

"OK, here goes. When I spoke to you last, I had said to you that Robin asked me to ask you for your forgiveness. Like I mentioned, after she had Ezra, she developed cancer in her right breast. The doctor felt that because it was caught early that she may have remained cancer-free. She did, for three years, and then the cancer returned. She ended up with a double mastectomy, and for the next year, she fought bravely, but the cancer spread to her liver, and eventually her whole body became comprised. About a month before she died, she said that she had to tell me something and begged me to forgive her and not to be angry with her. She said that she loved me, and she was sorry for what she did. Her words still echo within my mind to this day . . . *'Tony, I know my actions were wrong, but from the first day Maureen introduced me to you as her boyfriend, the way you smiled at me as you said hello, I had this instant attraction to you. At first, I tried to put it out my mind, and I tried subtly to see if you could have felt the spark, but I never got it. Then Maureen, she used to show off so much among the girls, it was "Tony did this" or "Tony did that," and she would say things like "That's my baby," or "Isn't my baby cute?" I know she couldn't have known how I felt, but every time she would act out and I would see you two together, I began to get jealous and felt that I was as good as her, so there is no reason why I could not have you instead.'"*

He stopped for a minute. I wasn't sure if he wanted to me confirm her comments on my actions; I shook my head.

"She was right, but I never suspected that she felt the way she did. She was my girlfriend, and that's what girlfriends do—they talk about their boyfriends." I actually felt annoyed at having to defend myself.

"Maureen," Tony continued, "I also have to say that apart from the time you introduced me to her and any time after I had seen her, she was never in my mind. I never gave her a second glance or a second thought.

Anyway, let me continue the story. As she continued to talk with me, she asked me if I recalled what happened the night I slept with her. I told her vaguely.

"Maureen, this is how it started for me. I had just walked outside and about to get in my car to run to the mall to pick up some ink for my printer. As I opened the car, up walks Robin. She asked me where I was going, and I told her. She asked if I could give her a ride to her cousin's house to pick up a parcel. She said that the cousin was supposed to have dropped it off for her but couldn't do it, and she was thinking of going over there to get it. I asked her where her cousin lived, and it turned out that she was at exit 31, and the mall was exit 32. I figured, it's all on my way, so I decided to take her. I knew the whole trip could have taken us less than an hour. I thought of calling you to tell you I was giving her a ride, but I figured I'd tell you later when I saw you. Following her directions, we arrived at the building, which was a small apartment complex. She asked me to come with her, as she may need help carrying the parcel or parcels. I was a little reluctant but decided, as I had come this far, I could as well help her. We walked up two flights of stairs and came to an apartment door. She rang the bell, no answer. She said that her cousin had given her a key from before and had told her that if she came and she wasn't home, just come in and the parcels will be on the table. She opened the door, and we both went inside. There were two boxes sitting on the table, and I stood there while she looked the boxes over. I saw her go into the fridge and took out a bottle and poured some of the liquid into two glasses. She walked up to me and said, *'You have to try this. It's the most incredible punch my grandmother makes. If she had to sell it, she will make millions.'* I shook my head, indicating that I didn't want any. *'Come on, believe me, it's very good, just try it, please.'*

"I took the glass from her. She, in the meantime, had drunk hers off. I put the glass to my lips, and I tasted it. It tasted good. I figured, let me just drink it to satisfy her so we could get out of here and I could go do what I got to do. I saw her lighting up a cigarette, and I remember thinking that I didn't even know she smokes, but I just wanted to go. Within minutes of finishing the punch, a feeling came over me. My knees started to feel wobbly. I saw Robin watching me. I started to turn for the door, and I felt her arms go around my waist, and she led me to the sofa to sit down. I must have passed out or something. I don't know if I was dreaming. It felt like I was in a movie, and I could feel myself walking in this strange place. It was a place I have never been before I found myself in this dimly lit room, I could smell the scent of flowers all around me and I remember making love to a woman. I couldn't see her face clearly, but there was something about her, the way she smelled, the way she caressed me, and I was loving her with a passion I didn't know I had in me. I felt as if I was drifting in and out of the consciousness not knowing where I was.

Eventually, my head cleared, and as I opened my eyes and my brain began to focus, I realized that I was naked. The room was semi dark, and I felt someone next to me. I turned my head and saw that it was Robin. I jumped out of the bed and started looking for my clothes. Robin got out the bed and turned on the light. I was panicking, 'What happened to me, Robin?' I shouted at her. 'Where are my clothes?' She stood there looking at me with this almost crazy smile on her face.

'Where are my clothes?' I demanded of her roughly. She pointed to them in a chair in the corner. I hastily put on my briefs and pants, followed by my shirt, pushed my feet in my shoes, and started for the door.

"'Tony,' she called after me, 'where are you going? Stay. You don't feel well.' I didn't reply. I found the front door and walked down the stairs. The blast of cool breeze to my face helped me revive a little. I couldn't figure out where I was. I felt as if I had lost my sense of direction. I found my car, got in, and sat for a few minutes in order to refocus. I looked at the clock. It said 11:00 p.m. Seven hours had gone by, and I had no recollection of them. I took my time, and I drove back to the dorm, stumbled into my room, closed the door, and collapsed on my bed. The next time I opened my eyes, it was 8:00 a.m. It took me about two days before I began to feel like myself again. I couldn't wrap my mind around what had happened to me. I wanted to tell you, but I was afraid because I myself wasn't sure what had happened. I went to the doctor the day after, and I tried to explain to him how I was feeling. He did a routine checkup, and he said that everything looked fine, that maybe I was stressed with finals coming up and finishing school and having to find a job, that all that may be a contributing factor. I know that wasn't it. I wanted to talk to Robin, but no matter where I looked, I couldn't find her, and I was too afraid to ask you if you had seen her.

That weekend, I came down to Brooklyn to talk to my mother about it, and she was alarmed and wanted to take me to another doctor, but I told her I was fine. My mother felt that she might have given me some type of drug and that I needed to keep far from that girl. My mother said that there had to be some Obeah involved. Her telling me that only made me more upset. I understood something of what Obeah is capable of doing. My mother got on my case, asking me how many times she has told me not to be too quick to eat and drink from people. People, she said, can hurt you—what goes into your system can destroy you.

"It was about two weeks before I saw Robin, and when I confronted her, she said she didn't know what I was talking about. Twice I tried to talk to her, and the last time, she said to me, '*If you don't stop bothering me, I am going to tell Maureen you are trying to seduce me.*' That scared the daylights out of me because I didn't want her to tell you something like that. I felt so guilty and worried about what had happened to me.

After that incident, I avoided her like the plague. A little over a month, I woke up one morning so nauseous. I started vomiting. I wondered if I had eaten something spoiled. I got over that. It happened again five days later. I started to get worried again. That same day, as I was leaving class, Robin walked up to me and said she had to talk to me. I turned and walked away from her, and she followed me. The next words she said to me hit me like a sledgehammer. *'Tony, stop, I am pregnant.'* I turned around to face her, my eyes not really seeing her. I would feel this sensation that hit me in the pit of my chest and rippled all the way to the bottom of my belly.

'What?' I practically shouted at her.

'I am expecting a baby,' she replied.

'What has that got to do with me?' I asked her, thinking to myself, this woman is crazy.

'It's your baby,' she answered roughly. *'Don't pretend you don't remember what you did.'*

'What did I do, Robin?'

She smiled this crooked smile, shaking her head, *'You made love to me at my cousin's house, you forget about that?'*

'Robin,' I said, 'what did you do to me?' What was in that punch?'

'I didn't do anything to you. You wanted me, you took me, and now I am pregnant.'

I looked at her, disgusted written all over my face. I turned my back without another word to her, and I walked away.

Robin said as I turned away, *'You cannot walk away from this. Sooner or later, you are going to have to deal with me and your child.'"*

Tony stopped talking, and he looked at me. I know I was sitting here transfixed, my mind processing at lightning speed all he was saying. I couldn't believe what I was hearing—could this be true? Is this what happened?

"Maureen, shall I continue? I know it's a bit much." He lifted his glass and drank some lemonade.

"It's OK, please continue." I was already in too deep; I had to hear the rest of it.

That weekend again, I came home to tell Mom what had happened. You know my mom was also easy for me to talk to. I feel closer to my mom than my father. I was in a desperate position because if the child was mine, I had to let my parents know what had happened, and telling my father was something I dread more than anything else in the world. When I told my mom what Robin said, she was livid. I then told her about you and that you were whom I loved and hoped to marry one day. She told me to go to you and tell you what was going on before you heard it from Robin or somebody else. I was going to tell you, but after my father got through with me, I felt so stupid—I wished I could have died right then.

He paused for a minute with both elbows on the table, his hands interlaced together. He put his face in his hands. He didn't speak for a minute, just shook his head, as if he was reliving the event. I reached over and touched his arm as if to say, 'It's all right, I understand.' He removed his hands from his face and took my hands.

"Thanks for caring. This is still very painful for me. I thought I could handle this but talking about it has opened up wounds that have not healed."

I nodded my head; I understood where he was coming from. I too have tried to bury that portion of my life.

"Anyway," he continued, "I sat down with my father and told him the whole story. He listened attentively, and he said to me, 'Did you sleep with this girl?'

I told him I believed so, but it was foggy to me. I explained the sequences of events as they had occurred.

'Well,' he said, 'the only thing to be done is for you to marry her so your child is legitimate.'

I was horrified. 'Marry her?' I found myself shouting.

'Yes, marry her,' my father responded harshly. 'How do you expect me, as a pastor, to counsel any family if my own family cannot do the right thing? You think I will be pleased if your sister got pregnant and the man walked away from her and left her with a child? No, my son, you have to do the right thing before God. From the beginning, I have talked to you and admonished you about premarital sex. You came up in this household being taught the word of God. I sent you away to college so you would become an educated black man who could work and take care of his family properly. You should be an example to your sisters and this family of how a young black man should conduct himself. You come from a proper family, and this is what you do? Then you come to me. What do you expect me to say? —no more than you have to do the right thing. I cannot let you embarrass me and the rest of our family."

Again, he stopped talking, the anguish showing so deeply in his face.

Oh my god, I was thinking, *this is unbelievable.* Maybe to someone else, they may say, all of this is too little too late, but sitting here with him, my inner being was moved by him, maybe because he was my first love, maybe, but I didn't think so. It was his whole demeanor; this had been a very traumatic experience for him, one that obviously he has not been able to get over yet.

As all of this was going through my mind, I was jarred back to reality by the voice of a little boy.

"Dad, where are you? I am home." I could hear the sound of the patter of little feet running toward us.

"I am over here, son," Tony replied.

The little one bounced into the room, dressed in a suit, as if he went to a church service or the like. He was followed by a middle-aged woman, also dressed as if she had been to church. He ran up to his father, who proceeded to lift him up, swinging him up and over his shoulders before setting him back to the ground.

"Hold on," Tony said, "mind your manners now. You didn't say hello to Miss Maureen."

"Hello, Miss Maureen. What are you doing here?"

"Ezra," his father said sternly, "Miss Maureen is my guest visiting me this evening."

Tony turned to face the woman who was standing here all smiles. "Aunt Mae, this is my friend Maureen Coleman. She reached out her hand to me as I did mine to her. We shook hands with the usual "nice to meet you" greeting.

"Come on, Ezra," Aunt Mae said, "let's get changed. It's going to be dinnertime soon."

"Miss Maureen," Ezra said, "I will be right back. He turned and followed Aunt Mae out the room.

"He is adorable," I said.

"Thank you. He is the reason I get out of bed in the mornings. He is who keeps me going at times when I want to give up."

"In the park the other day, Tony, you said that he should have been our son. What did you mean by that?"

"I meant," he answered, "that if my dreams and hopes for us to have married and become a family had worked out, he would have been our first child. What his mother did to me was something I never saw coming. I grew up so sheltered, and in church, I never had street smarts, so when all of this came on me suddenly, it left me reeling for years. I wasn't ready to be a father, but I had to learn fast. I can't hold any of this against him. He's an innocent kid, but he is also my flesh and blood. I pray that I could be the kind of father he could come to and always feel that I am there for him to be able to help him in any crisis. I would like him to have the kind of father I always wanted."

"Tony, what you have shared with me is unbelievable. I would have never thought for a minute that all of this went on. When you broke up with me, I felt that you cheated on me with Robin and this was what you wanted. This is like something of out a novel, or some dark movie. It boggles the mind."

"Maureen, believe me when I say I never cheated on you with anyone. I never looked at Robin twice. I just know she was one of your friends, and that was all I knew. What I thought of as a good deed by giving her a ride almost became a death sentence for me. Let me finish this off before Ezra gets back. Robin confessed to me that she had planned the whole incident. It wasn't her cousin's apartment—it was a place she had rented to carry out her scheme. She said she needed a place where she would not be disturbed so as to give her the time she needed. The drink she gave me was drugged to get me incapacitated, and once she had me, she said that she followed the instructions given to her by her grandmother to put me in that trance I was in. She said that she was born with a gift, and she was like her grandmother who could make portions and tell fortunes. She wanted to get pregnant because she figured if she did, I would marry her, and she would have me all to herself.

The day she confessed all this to me, I was in a state of disbelief. I knew she had done something to me—I just didn't know what. It had tortured me for years. I questioned my sanity and relived it over and over, looking for something that I may have missed. I told her that she had my forgiveness, but more importantly, I hope she begs God for his forgiveness.

When I left the hospital that evening, I sat in my car in the parking lot and cried. It hurt me so much as I realized that she was capable of such deviousness, and she took five years of my life away from me. I know that I have survived this because of God's grace and mercy because I know that our God never leaves us or forsakes us. Two weeks later, she was dead."

I sat there, stunned by all that he revealed. I wasn't sure how I felt— no that wasn't true, I was angry, I felt betrayed by a so-called friend; and you know what is ironic—I have suffered just as much as Tony did from the actions of this woman. Can you image how this woman has impacted our life?

"Miss Maureen,"—Ezra came running— "look at my Iron Man." He came up to me to show me his toy. "See, he can talk." He pushed a button, and the toy said, "I am Iron Man."

"Wow, he is great," I answered, putting a smile on my face. I pushed the negative thoughts as far away as I could and decided to respond to this dear child.

"Do you want to see my Wrestlers? I have a lot of them. Come, let me show you." He started to take my hand.

"OK, Ezra, calm down a minute. Miss Maureen is going to come in a few minutes. Why don't you go and get them all together and I will bring her?"

"OK, Daddy," he said and ran out the room.

"I hope you don't mind seeing his wrestlers. He's not used to having visitors, so he is excited."

"It's fine. After all I have heard this evening, the laughter of a child is soothing to my ears." I needed a happy thought right about now.

"Let me say one last thing—you have no idea what talking to you has done for me. There is so much gratitude in me right now for you. Thank you, Maureen."

"It's quite a bit. I know I will be thinking about this for a while, but I am glad I came. This has finally answered many questions for me."

"Let me take you up to Ezra's room so you can see his wrestlers. Thank you for being willing to humor a little boy."

I stood up, and he took me by the arm to show me the way upstairs. I went along, but inside, my emotions were ranging from anger to sadness, to disbelief, and back to anger again. I had to give myself a quick check. *Don't let this swallow you. You are not the only victim here. Believe it or not, all three of you are victims. Father God, give me the strength to calm down.*

I arrived at the room door, and Ezra ran over to take my hand and pulled me in.

"Look, Miss Maureen, I set them all up. See, I have the ring also so we can have a wrestling match."

His father looked at me, and I at him. What do you do with this ball of energy? I thought to myself. You know what, I decided, I am going to have fun with him. So, I got on the carpeted floor and chose a wrestler to put in the ring. "OK," I said, "let's get ready to rumble."

"See," I said to Tony, laughing, "I know something about wrestling."

"I see," he said, "I will be your cheering crowd."

So, the match began!

Chapter 10

"Thank you for coming, Maureen. This has been a most amazing evening. Never in all my thoughts did I think this evening would have turned out so wonderful. Maureen, please allow me to say this: you are beautiful in so many ways."

"Ah, Tony, thank you. I had a great evening with you and Ezra."

"Please drive safely and call me as soon as you get home so I'll know you are in safe."

"Will do," I responded. "Thanks again." I got in the car, and he closed the door for me. I started the car, and I drove off.

He was right; this was one amazing evening. At first, I was uncertain as to whether I should have gone. After all these years, could Tony have told me anything that would erase the pain and heartache I felt when we broke up? Then I wondered why he felt obligated to keep his promise to Robin when he knew he would have to talk to me.

The story he told me, as incredible as it sounded, I believe he was telling the truth. I know that there are a lot of things that happen to people that most would call unexplained phenomenon. My gut instincts had me believing him, but I was going to check out his story. I arrived home, and once inside, I called Tony to say I was in. He thanked me again and wished me a good night. As he hung up, he said, "I'll call you tomorrow, is that OK?"

"That's fine," I replied. "Talk to you then. Good night."

I sat on the sofa for a while, reliving the evening. How could Robin have been so devious as to trick Tony like that? Was that girl right in her head to calculate and carry out a plan that affected so many people's lives? Tony and his family, my life, and then to use a child in this wild scheme of hers, what kind of woman does shit like that? Maybe behind her pretty face lurked a dark heart. Who's to say what her whole mental makeup was? She had become obsessed with my guy, and she systematically planned and executed a plan to get him, and she went to great lengths to make sure that it wouldn't fail by having a child to hold on to him.

Little Ezra, such a darling boy, there is no way you could hold what his mother did against him. He too at this point is without mother, and it's plain to see how much he wants a mother's love. A smile came to my face as I thought about how the evening evolved. We started out playing with the wrestlers and ended up putting a big jigsaw puzzle together. I cannot remember if I ever had fun like that; just the way the three of us were on the floor looking for pieces and laughing, getting excited at finding a piece you needed, made it fun, sort of what I envision a loving family might do on a Sunday evening. Just as we finished assembling it, Aunt Mae had called to say dinner was ready. At that point, Tony looked at me and said,

"Maureen, please stay and have dinner with us." Before he could finish his sentence, Ezra was next to me.

"Please, Miss Maureen, stay for dinner. Aunt Mae is making barbecue ribs today—yum, they are my favorite."

"Oh, I don't know, I didn't plan on dinner," I replied.

"I know it's sudden, but if you can," Tony said, "it would make me and Ezra very happy."

"Yes, Miss Maureen," Ezra chimed in, "it will make me very happy."

"OK," I said, "I'll stay for dinner."

"Ezra," his father said, "go and tell Aunt Mae that Miss Maureen is staying for dinner."

"OK," he said and flew out of the room as fast as his little feet took him.

"He is such a ball of energy," I said.

"You better believe it—his father confirmed."

Tony got up from the floor and reached over with both hands and raised me up. For what seemed like an eternity, he stood there, holding both my hands, his eyes looking deeply into my face. I felt my heart start to race. When we were in school, he had that boyish look to him; but now he was a mature man, his eyes, a light shade of brown, a moustache that covered his upper lip, the face of a handsome man looking at me.

"Dad, Miss Maureen, dinner's ready, come on," Ezra shouted from the bottom of the stairs. His calling came just in time; it felt as if we were locked in a mini time warp just looking so deeply into each other's face.

Tony let go of my hand and politely said, "After you," indicating for me to walk ahead.

"Before I go," I said, "I would like to wash my hands?"

"Sure," he said and showed me to hallway bathroom. I washed my hands, dabbed my face with the damp paper towel, and walked out.

"Wait for me while I wash mine also," Tony said.

I stood outside and waited for him. We then proceeded to the dining room. He pulled out a chair for me to sit. He sat at the head of the table, me to his right, Ezra to his left, and Aunt Mae sat next to Ezra. We held hand for grace, with Tony blessing the food.

"Amen!" said Aunt Mae. "Tony, when are you going to start helping your father preach down at the church?"

"Aunt Mae, you know I ain't no preacher. I just pray good, but that's from all the years of listening to Daddy praying."

"I still think you got it. Maureen," she said, "where do you know Tony from?"

"We went to the same college," I answered.

"Oh, you're Maureen, she said. Her voice carrying a hint of realization, of something she knew before. After that, she didn't say anything else.

I looked over at Tony; he had an almost uncomfortable look to his face, but he quickly livened up and said, "Pass the yams, Aunt Mae," which she did.

"So, Ezra," Tony said, "how was the play?" Ezra started telling us about the play as we enjoyed barbecue spareribs, yams, collard greens, and vegetable rice. The meal was delicious.

As I thought about it, it looks as if Aunt Mae knew about me. The look on her face as she came to a realization that I was Maureen made me believe that she may know of me and what happened to her nephew.

After dinner, Tony took me on a tour of the house. It was a two-story house with three bedrooms on the second floor. On the first floor were the living room, a formal dining room, and a kitchen. The porch, which was the enclosed area off the kitchen, had a door that opened to steps that led to the backyard. In the basement area, he had a laundry room, the boiler room, and then he had a room set up with big screen TV, stereo equipment, and a leather sofa. This, he said, was his playroom, where he watched his games in surround sound and had the guys over to watch special games. The house was well furnished, beautifully decorated, and well kept. As he showed me around, we left Ezra and Aunt Mae upstairs. I asked him how he manages everything. He said that Aunt Mae has been a lifesaver for him. After Robin's death, he wanted to come back to New York to be close to his family to help him raise Ezra. Aunt Mae is his mother's sister, and she told him she will help him with Ezra.

As luck would have it, Aunt Mae lives two doors away, and when the owner of this house decided to sell in order to relocate, Aunt Mae was able to help him negotiate a good price, having been friends with the owner for all the years she lived on the block. Like he said, Aunt Mae has been a real lifesaver for him and Ezra.

So many times, during the course of the evening, as I looked in his face, I could detect the sadness in him. I can't begin to imagine what his life was like with Robin, but I am sure he had to feel cheated and trapped. Cheated because his plans for a life with me were snatched away before they even had a chance to develop and blossom. Trapped, because he had a strong sense of obligation to his father, which superseded his own desires.

I know that he would not have left her because I am sure his father must have preached to him about the sanctities of marriage. Some may say that he was his own man and did not have to listen or do what his father said. But at the time this happened, he was like a child, still under the rules of his father and being instilled with the doctrine of honor to the family and not to disgrace them. For him to have gone through this, I saw him as a strong man with high regards for his family and their values. Not many men would have done what he did.

One other thing that I noticed was the tenderness in his eyes toward me. I felt as if he was fighting the urge to kiss me as he held the car door open for me to get into my car. I could feel the electricity that pulsated from him and threatened to engulf me. I was glad that he stood his ground and did not yield to his desire. I wanted to take the time to see if I could love him again. If what he told me was true, then he didn't leave me because he wanted to, but he left because he felt he had no choice.

I wondered what I would have done if he had told me, like his mother told him to do. Maybe the outcome might have been different. I got up from the sofa, took my shower, and prepared for bed. A new day begins tomorrow; I will see what it brings.

The next day, Tony did call after work, still thanked me for yesterday, and invited me to his father's church on Sunday. He said that the church would be celebrating his father's thirty years as minister of the church.

"Maureen," he said, "I would really appreciate it if you could come with me and Ezra. After service, there will be a luncheon, and I would love to introduce you to Mom. She has heard so much about you from Ezra. You are all he talks about."

"Really?" I smiled. I know he couldn't see it over the phone, but Ezra was such a heart stealer. "Is he really talking about me?"

"He sure is. He told Mom that you are coming back to play with him and that you are going to help him put together another puzzle."

"Oh my," I said, "I guess I'm in trouble now. Seriously, Tony, I don't know if I am ready to meet your parents. I am trying not to overthink this, but can I give you an answer by Friday? Please let me think about it for a day or two."

"Sure, Maureen," he said. "I don't want to do anything that makes you uncomfortable. Whatever you decide, I will respect your decision."

"Thanks. Say hello to Ezra for me."

"Will do," he said. "We'll speak hopefully on Friday."

"Yes," I replied, "on Friday. Bye."

I hung up the phone. *Wow, he wants me to go to church with him to meet his parents. What does this all mean in English?* I thought to myself.

I decided that this was my time to call my mom. I really need a mother-and-daughter talk, or a woman-to-woman talk from someone who was older and wiser. I called up my mom and asked her if she was busy the next evening, as I wanted to discuss something with her. She said she wasn't and that I should come by after work.

Jacqueline Donna Coleman (Jackie, as she is called by family and friends) is my mother. As I have gotten older, I have grown to appreciate her wisdom. I am sure we all can recount so many incidences growing up when we did not want to hear what our mothers had to say. We couldn't wait to grow up to get from under her rule. It's only as the years have rolled along and we have experienced life that we realize she knew what she was talking about.

In our household, she was our disciplinarian, our teacher, our cook; she was someone that was always there. As a child growing up, I was deathly afraid of the lightning and thunder especially those loud claps that seem as if it would fall out the sky and crush you into bits. When that lightning lit up the sky and the thunder rolled, I could be found next to Mom; no matter where she was in the house, I was going to find her. Some people think I look like my mother.

Now at fifty-two years old, she still looks pretty good. She and my dad had started dating when Mom was twenty-one, and they got married two years later. They've been married close to thirty years. I know that they have had their share of disagreements. On many occasions, try as they did to hide it from us kids, I could tell when there was tension between them. I have seen Dad sleeping on the sofa, and I have seen them barely uttering a word between them; but through it all, they have stayed together and made it work.

Ezra Paul Coleman, my dad, is one hardworking, no-nonsense, loving man. Back in the day, he was so athletic—in a way, he still is but I guess these days, he paces himself. If you saw pictures of my parents when they were younger, they could rival any Hollywood couple. Now with everyone grown, they just enjoy themselves. Every so often, I will hear Mom say that they are taking a trip somewhere for the weekend. I had mentioned Tony to Mom maybe on two occasions. I never told her that I was dating Tony because back then, I know I would have gotten the lecture about my studies coming first and boyfriend later. I didn't think she minded me dating, but not to get serious. For her, I needed to concentrate on earning my degree. I wondered what she will say when I recount the relationship I had with Anthony. I had not gone into a lot of details with her regarding my breakup with James the little that I told her, I could see from her expression that she was disappointed on how it all worked out. She had liked James, maybe because he was the first and only man that I brought home and introduced to my parents. Also, James was quite the dashing prince. I believed my mother admired him, the way he carried himself as a young black man, and I know she was hoping it would have worked out for us.

On several occasions, she had asked me when we were planning to get married. She really didn't care too much for us living together, as she said in one of her famous sayings, "Why is a man going to buy the goat if he can get the milk free?"—meaning, of course, what would motivate James to marry when he is enjoying all the comforts of a married man without being married? I, on the other hand, wanted to give it a try; well, we saw what happened to that.

While I wanted to hear my mother's opinion on this whole situation, I wondered if she would think me crazy for even caring, if what Tony told me was true or even possible. I have just barely gotten over James and the way he walked out my life. Now Tony with this messed-up story of witchcraft, planning, and plotting—should I even be entertaining all this craziness? The only thing I was going on was my gut feelings. Listening to Tony, I was convinced that he didn't make up this story, and then there is Ezra; my spirit took to him so easily. Yes, he is Robin's child, but he is also Tony's. I can't hold anything that Robin did against him. If I had a son, I would want him to be just like little Ezra. Maybe someday, I'll have my baby, and God will bless me with a bundle of joy that will be just as precious as Ezra.

In the meantime, I was prepared to listen attentively to what advise my mother had to give, because right about now, I need to let myself heal before I think of getting involved so deeply again with someone else, and that includes Tony, especially Tony. As I thought about it, I was more hurt with the breakup of me and Tony than me and James. It's not that it didn't hurt me, but the relationship with James had started to decline, and over the months, I saw it gradually disintegrating. Tony, on the other hand, my first love, when he told me he could not be seeing me anymore, and then I heard that he married Robin, the suddenness of it all tore me to pieces.

Sometimes, I wondered how I made it. I went through the motions of functioning, but I was numb for months. I wished he had listened to his mother and had come and put his cards on the table; at least I would have had an explanation. Oh well, I'll hear what Mom has to say, and then I will come to a decision.

Chapter 11

I sat across the kitchen table from Mom. "The soup is great," I said to her. "You always make the best soup. You need to teach how to make it one day."

"Whenever you are ready," she replied, "but you will have to come and watch me and take notes, because I do not measure anything. I just know how much of everything to put in."

"Mom," I said, "I want to talk to you about something that's important to me." She looked up from her food, her eyes focusing in on my face, and I could see concern beginning to spread across her face.

"It's nothing to worry about. I just need to hear your opinion on what I am about to tell you."

"OK, I'll do my best." For the next half an hour, I related to her how I met Tony and what happened between us and what he told me that Robin did to him. She listened very attentively, interrupting on a couple of occasions with words of surprise such as "wow," "oh dear," and a shaking of the head followed by "my, my, my." At the end, she asked me, "Maureen, do you believe his story?"

"In my gut, I believe he is telling the truth, but are things like what he said Robin did possible? He said his mother felt that Obeah was involved—what does that mean?"

"His mother may be right," she replied. "There is more to this world than what we see physically. There is a spiritual side too, and there are people who make it their study and have knowledge that can be used for good or bad. Robin's grandmother was obviously one of those people who knew herbs and spells most likely passed down through their family. There is knowledge that came with us when we left Africa as slaves. So, what happened to him is very possible.

My mother used to tell us things that her mother told her about people using Obeah to get men to marry them. As funny as some of the tales were, they were true things that happened to people. But now, Maureen, what is he hoping for by telling you this story?"

"I am really not sure," I replied. "At least, I believe he is hoping that I will forgive him, as Robin asked him to have me forgive her."

"Do you think he is still in love with you?" She hesitated for a minute, looking squarely in my face. "Are you in love with him, or would you consider getting involved again with him?"

"Mom, I really don't know. Right now, I feel a little overwhelmed with all this information. If what he said is true, then he is as much a victim of this as I am. I am so mad at Robin. Over the years, I had buried her and him somewhere in the recesses of my brain and tried to go on with my life, but now that he has come and reopened everything, and hearing what she did, if she were alive, I would want to beat the crap out of her for her deviousness. How does a person become so desperate and conniving? Does love drive a person to this type of behavior?"

"No," she replied, "that is not love—that's obsession. In Robin's case, it could have also been fueled by jealousy and a feeling of entitlement. She probably figured, why should you get such a bright and handsome man? She felt she was the one who should have him and not you, so she set out to take him from you. You know, something similar to this happened to me and your father."

"What? Really?"

"Yeah, I must have been going out with your father for about a year, and I had a coworker—that we were best buddies. As a matter of fact, some people in the office used to refer to us as Batman and Robin, because where you saw me, you saw her. We would take our lunch together and socialize on some occasions. While we sat having lunch, stupid me would relay to her how good your father was in bed. I would be telling her all my little intimate details. She would listen and laugh at some things or make little smart comments.

This went on for a while. Eventually, I got transferred to another unit, and we started seeing less and less of each other. When your father and I decided to get married, I sent her an invitation to the wedding, and she responded that she was unable to attend, as she would be out of town and not available.

Years later, your father and I were talking one day, and her name came up. I saw him smiling, and I asked him if I had said something funny. He looked at me, and he said,

"'I can tell you this now cause you my wife and you not going anywhere."

At that point, he had my undivided attention. He said that before we had gotten married, one day, he had run into her on the street, and she asked him if he wouldn't mind giving her a ride home. He gave her the ride home and he helped her carry her bags into the apartment. He said once inside the door, she hugged him and tried to kiss him. He said he was a little taken aback and gently held her at arm's length while asking her why.

She told him she was in love with him, and had heard so much about him, and how great he was in bed, and she wanted him.

Your father said he told her he loved me, and if she knows what was best for her, she better forget about him, because if I ever found out that she wanted to take him away, there is no telling what I would do.

He said he left and decided not to tell me anything, because knowing me, I would have probably slapped the shit of her for her rudeness."

"Wow, Mom, oh my god! Some of these women out here crazy as hell, and bold too".

"Girl, your father knows me—I don't be playing that shit. I have calmed down over the years, but no other woman better not mess with my man—go find your own. You know my grandmother had a saying: 'High wind know where old house live.'"

"What does that mean?" I asked her.

"In other words," she replied, "some people know whom they can mess with. If you were like me back in the day, she won't have messed with Tony. But all that is now water under the bridge. The question is, what are you going to do now?"

"Like I said, I am trying to work it out."

"You said he invited you to church on Sunday. I think you should go. There must be a reason why he wants you to meet his parents. I know you think I have all these sayings, but truly, God moves in a mysterious way, his wonders to perform. Keep an open mind and take it slowly, one day at a time."

"I told him I will call him on Friday with an answer, so I have until then to think it all over."

"OK, let me know what you decide." As we finished our talk, my brother, Charlie, walked in.

"Hi Mo Mo"—that was his nickname for me.

"Hi there. Long time no see," I replied. "You don't even call me to see how I am doing."

"You're right, sis. Sorry, I will do better, but now also, you would pick up the phone and call me too?"

"OK, true, true, I'll do better too," I answered back.

"What's for dinner, Mom?" he said.

"I made some chicken soup. Do you want me to fix you a bowl?"

"Sure thing," he replied as he turned to walk away, I assume going to his room.

"You're still pampering him?" I asked. "You know any woman he marries is going to have a hard time with him because he is going to expect her to baby him like you do."

"I don't think so. She doesn't have to baby him, but she should treat him right. Take some advice from a woman who has been a wife for years. It's the little things you do for your husband that makes him feel special and wanted—that keeps your marriage alive. It's not about who does what, or who should or shouldn't do what, but it's about you two caring for each other and doing things for each other in a caring and loving way. You should have your home so organized that your husband looks forward at the end of the day to be with you, that there is no place that he would rather be than in his own home with his wife."

"You must be on to something. You have stayed married long enough," I replied. "Don't you think that things are different now? Marriages don't seem to last as long as they used to."

"Well," she responded, "that's because some people come into a marriage with preconceived notion of what married life will be. Every relationship requires constantly working at it and readjustments. It's not going to work if the two people are pulling in two different directions and no one is willing to back down every now and then for the sake of harmony."

"Well, if I get married, I will certainly take your advice."

"If you get married?" she said, with a big smile on her face. "It's more like *when* you get married. You'll get married—just wait, it's coming fast."

I had spent a very pleasant evening with Mom. I was amazed at the way she took all the information in stride, and not once did she show any disapproval for all the things, I related that I did. I think she realized that all of it was in the past and everything still worked out in the end. I finished school, I got my degree, and I overcame all the heartache and kept on going. There was a look of pride on her face as we chitchat a while longer on various family issues, to see that I was able to stay strong, and she wasn't even aware that all of this had gone on in my life.

As I got ready to leave, my dad came in, and that delayed me even longer. There was no way, once he came, that I could just up and leave; he had to have his time with me. By the time all the talking had finished, it was ten fifteen, and Charlie said he would drive me home. He didn't get any argument from me; I was perfectly happy to be taken to my door. With hugs and kisses to Mom and Dad, I got in the car, and he drove me home.

Once at home, I was ready for my shower and just couldn't wait to settle into bed. It was a time to reflect on what Mom had to say and also to think about Tony.

He must still feel something for me. But what do I feel? Should I throw all that has happened behind my back and try to start anew? Would it work? We are now two grown people with more life experience than when we were back in college. Then there was little Ezra—could I learn to love him, knowing that he will be a constant reminder of what his mother did to me?

If I wanted to be part of Tony's life, it would mean having to love and raise his child as my own. I want a child, but do I want somebody else's child?

Also, this invite for Sunday and having to meet his parents, am I being invited to see if I would meet with their approval? I have already formulated in my mind an opinion of Tony's father. I felt from what Tony told me that he didn't support his son when he came to him for help.

To insist that Tony marry so as to keep him looking as if his family was in order, I felt, was selfish of him.

What if Robin hadn't died? —that meant that Tony would have been stuck for life in a marriage that he was tricked into. Because of his loyalty to his father, and the responsibility to keep his family's name honorable he would have had to live with a woman whom he didn't love.

I wanted to meet his father, because believe it or not, he was a key player in my life, even though I didn't know it at the time. His decision changed the course of Tony's and my life.

As I lay there thinking, my mind drifted back to the Sunday I was at his house, when we were assembling the jigsaw puzzle.

That evening, we felt like a family; everything felt so right, but I am so afraid to get my hopes up and then have them crash to the ground. Sitting and talking to him, seeing the care he exhibited toward Ezra, evoked feelings of tenderness within me. There is a sensitivity within me that I feel toward him. It felt as if he was reaching out to me, but who's to say that I am right? The cost of being wrong would be so painful. "OK, Maureen," I said to myself, "enough! You have had a long day, and tomorrow is work. Go to sleep. All the answers you need will be provided to you—just believe."

Chapter 12

I was ready; Tony should be here any minute. I looked at myself one last time in the mirror. I looked pretty good, if I am to say so myself. I had decided to accept Tony's invitation to his father's anniversary service and luncheon. I had ordered an outfit from a catalog, and I prayed that it would be as beautiful as the picture. I wasn't disappointed; it was perfect.

It was a soft lime-green two-piece skirt suit and a matching hat. I accessorized it with a silver necklace, earrings, and bracelet. As I looked in the mirror, my mind drifted back to the conversation I had with Tony on Friday. When I told him I would attend, I could hear him exhale as if he had been holding his breath, hoping that I was not going to disappoint him.

"Thank you, Maureen," he said. "You have made me so happy, and I am sure Ezra is going to be just as excited when I tell him you are coming. The service starts at 11:00 a.m., so I will pick you up by 10:15 a.m. That should give us enough time to get there, find parking, and get to our seats."

"Tony," I said, "I could meet you there. You don't have to come over here for me."

"No, it is only correct and gentlemanly that I pick you up—you are my guest. Plus, Maureen, I want to do this. It's my way to say thank you."

"OK, I will be ready for ten fifteen, Sunday morning."

The ringing of the doorbell startled me out of my thoughts; that has to be Tony. I took up my handbag and walked to the door. I opened the front door to the street, and there he was. The look in his eyes told me he liked what he saw.

"Good morning, my dear. You look beautiful." He reached up and took my hand and held it to his lips, kissing the back of my hand.

"Thank you," I said. "You look quite handsome yourself."

"Why, thank you, Ma'am." He offered me his arm and walked me to the car. He opened the passenger side door for me and waited for me to sit down before closing the door.

The church was on Thomas Boyland Avenue. As we drove up, we were lucky to find a parking within the block. We walked up to the church. The sign on the front said "Tabernacle of Praise, the Church of the Living God. Joseph M. Bradley, Senior Pastor." It listed the time of services and the days. Tony opened the door for me, and I stepped in. It was beautiful inside. I estimated it would hold about a two hundred people. The pulpit area was decorated with large vases of flowers. All around, members were coming in and taking their seats, some of them beautifully dressed. Many nodded and smiled as they passed by with a greeting of "good morning" or "grace and peace." Tony took my hand and led me to the front.

The choir members started to file in. We stopped in front of two people; I knew this had to be his mom and dad. "Mom, Dad, this is Maureen," he said, his smile lighting up his whole face. "Maureen, these are my parents, Rev. Dr. Joseph Bradley and Mrs. Marion Bradley." His father extended his hand, taking my hand and shaking firmly.

"Nice to meet you, Maureen. I have heard a lot about you. It's a pleasure to finally meet you."

"Thank you, sir," I said.

"Please, everyone calls me Pastor, and it has become my name." In the seconds that he held my hand, I looked at him; so here he was in the flesh, the man who made Tony marry Robin. He was about six feet, receding hair line, looked like an older version of Tony, glasses and a pleasant smile.

"OK, Pastor," I said, as I turned by attention to his wife.

His mom approached me next, and I extended my hand; she took it but then pulled me into her for a hug.

"Maureen, you are beautiful. I am so happy to finally meet you. I have not been able to hear my ears in the past week for your name. All Ezra talks about is Miss Maureen. You got a friend there for life."

"Thank you, Mrs. Bradley."

"Please," she said, "call me Marion. I am so looking forward to chatting with you." As she turned to walked away, being signaled by a member, I thought to myself that there is such a feeling of warmth that radiates from her. She is shorter than me, with broad hips and a little busty. Under her hat, I could see the gray streaks in her hair, but she was well put together; she looked every bit the "first lady" of the church.

By then, Pastor Bradley had excused himself and ascended the pulpit. The musicians started to play, and the whole church started singing. We sat in the first row, and as I looked to my left, who were sitting next to me but Aunt Mae and Ezra.

Right away, Ezra came and sat next to me, taking my hand. I reached over and gave him a kiss on his cheek, and he just smiled. For the next hour and a half, I sang, prayed, and got caught up in the music. The choir was fantastic.

Pastor Bradley preached a sermon that had the church on fire. I couldn't remember the last time I went to a church where I felt like I was in God's presence. When he did an altar call, I thought of going, but I couldn't get out of my seat. All sorts of things started filling my mind: Robin, Tony, his father's actions, James—was I ready to give my life to God? Would they think I was doing it to impress them? I sat in my seat and prayed silently for God to calm my mind.

At the conclusion of the service, Tony said that we would be going downstairs to the banquet. He held my hand, and Ezra held the other hand. Once downstairs, before I sat down, Tony walked me over to a young woman holding a baby and a man whom I assume was husband or related somehow. He introduced me to his sister Vivian and her husband, Rodney. They had a six-month-old baby girl, Brianana.

As we stood there, another young woman talked up to Tony and threw her arms around him, hugging him tightly. He hugged her in return and said to her,

"This is Maureen," indicating to me.

"Oh, Maureen, nice to see you," and she in turn gave me a big hug.

"This is my baby sister," he started to say.

"I ain't no baby," she interrupted, turning to him.

"OK, whatever you say," he answered. "Maureen, this is Shondell, my sister."

"Happy to meet you, Shondell," I said. For a minute, it seemed as if I was surrounded by his family and all eyes were on me. Apparently, everyone had heard of me.

As we stood there, Mrs. Bradley walked up and asked everyone to take their seats as the program was about to begin. Again, I sat next to Tony, and the remainder of the table was filled with his two sisters, and Rodney, Aunt Mae and Ezra, and two other ladies who were later introduced as Pastor Bradley's two nieces.

The program began, and for the next three hours, we listened to a history of the church and the accomplishments of Pastor Bradley. I must say that I was impressed with his involvement in the community, especially his ministry of working with juvenile offenders and the outreach program he had in the church for the youth of the area.

We were treated to several solos and a performance by the praise dancers of the church. Between all the speeches and performances, lunch was served. We had a choice of baked chicken or fried fish. I took the fried fish with the red skin potatoes and string beans. Tony had the baked chicken with yellow rice and string beans. Dessert was a choice of red velvet cake, plain cake, and ice cream. I took the red velvet with a scoop of ice cream. I enjoyed my meal.

As the program came to a close, Pastor Bradley thanked the congregation for all that they had done over the years to help him realize the success that the various ministries have enjoyed.

Several members of the congregation made presentations to him. He thanked and acknowledged the hard work, contribution, and dedication of his wife of thirty-five years. That brought a standing ovation from all present. As Mrs. Bradley stood next to him, he reached over and hugged her, giving her a kiss on the lips, which brought another round of applause from all assembly.

As he finished his speech, Tony and his two sisters got up and approached the podium. Tony took the microphone, and with his sisters on either side of him, he said,

"Mom, Dad, today is a special day for both of you. Mom, you have stood by Dad from the day he started. You recognized his calling, and you knew your place was beside him as he began his ministry for God. Today, thirty-five years later, you are still here standing faithfully by his side. Dad, as a boy growing up, I could not understand the level of commitment and leadership you had to your family and the church, but today as a man, I understand, and I am here to tell you today, Dad, that I have never been so proud to be your son as I am right now."

I could hear the emotion in his voice, and I pray for his strength at this time because I knew somewhat how deeply this was touching him. He was silent for what seemed like a long time, and I could sense the emotional distress he was in. Shondell recognized what was going on, and she came up to him, hugged him, and took the mike from him and continued,

"Mom, Dad, you both have worked so hard, hardly ever taking any real vacations, but all that is going to change," she added with a chuckle, which eased the silence and brought a few chuckles from the audience. "From the three of us, your loving children, we are happy and proud to present you with this gift of our love and esteem. It is a fourteen-day trip to Israel and the Holy Land." The cheering started. "Hold on, everyone, let me finish this. Mom and Dad, we want you to see firsthand the land that Jesus walked, to be able to see Calvary and all the places as recorded in the Bible."

The cheering was thunderous, and I could see the tears start to run down the face of Mrs. Bradley. Pastor Bradley was clearly emotionally affected, but he held his composure. The applause subsided, and the three of them returned to their seats.

As Tony sat down next to me, I could see the red in his eyes, and I reached over and took his hand, squeezing it and smiling. I mouthed the words to him, "It's OK."

He responded by squeezing my hand and said, "Thank you." The program closed, and people started to leave. We sat for a while as people continued to chat with each other, and Tony took the opportunity to talk to his two cousins who came up from Harrisburg for this occasion. Mrs. Bradley approached me as I sat there, waiting for Tony, who was stopped by members of the church who wanted to talk to him.

"Maureen," she said, "I would love for us to have lunch one day. Would you mind coming to visit with me?"

"Oh, thank you. I would love to come. Just let me know when."

"OK, great," she said. "Is it OK if I get your number from Tony to give you a call?"

"Sure, that would be fine," I answered.

"All right, I'll call a day next week. Thank you for coming. I am so happy to have finally met you. We have a lot to talk about."

I smiled. "OK, I will look forward to your call and lunch." She left, and Tony came back to my side, and we started heading for the door.

Out of nowhere, Ezra, who, once everything ended, had gone over by some of his little friends, and they were running amok and getting underfoot as the cleanup started. He was finally reined in by Aunt Mae, who herself was heading for the door.

"Miss Maureen, are you coming to my house to play with me?" I looked at Tony; he answered for me.

"Not today, Ezra. It's been a long day. She will come another day."

At this point, I chimed, "Yes, Ezra, I will come another day, I promise you." I reached over and gave him a hug and a kiss to the cheek.

"OK," he said grudgingly, "what day?"

"Daddy is going to tell you when soon, I promise"

"OK, bye," he said as Aunt Mae held on to him as she continued to the door.

Part of me felt a little sad; I hated to disappoint him, but so much was at stake right now. I couldn't endear myself into his life, and I didn't know if I would become part of it. If I had to leave, it would break his little heart; he had already lost his mom, maybe he was too young to understand the full effect of it, but I am sure he feels like something is missing in his life.

We drove home. Tony seemed to be deep in thought. I know the speech he gave had stirred up emotions in him; I just wasn't aware how deep they might be. When we arrived at my door, he parked and came around to open the car door for me. As I got out, I looked at him and asked him if he would like to come in.

"Sure," he replied.

"Would you like something to drink?" I asked him once we were inside the living room.

"A glass of wine would be nice if you have it." I took two glasses and partly filled them, handing one to Tony and holding on to the other one for myself.

"Cheers," I said, "and welcome."

"Thank you. You have a nice place here. Thank you for inviting me in."

"Please make yourself at home. You welcomed me into your home. It's only fitting that I do the same."

"Did you enjoy yourself today? It was a bit long," he said.

"I enjoyed every minute of it," I responded. "I met your parents and family, the service was great, and the program was excellent. Clearly your father is well loved by his congregation and respected in the community."

"Yes, he is," he answered, his face taking on a deep-in-thought look.

"Tony," I said, "was it difficult for you today as you spoke about your father and being proud to be his son?"

"Yes, it was difficult for me. For years, I felt like he had betrayed me and has no trust in me. When I needed him the most, he wasn't there for me. It took me a long time to try to see things from his perspective. The first couple of years of my marriage, I went through the motions of trying to live. Robin knew I didn't love her. I was torn between a sense of loyalty to my father and his position in the community, and my own feelings, which were suppressed because of the position I found myself in. Having to find a job and start to care for a family came on me suddenly—I really wasn't prepared. If you are with someone that you love, and the two of you work together to accomplish your goal, the task doesn't seem as taxing."

I looked at him; there is so much hurt in his eyes. I wondered how he has been able to cope with all of this.

"Maureen, thank you so much for coming today. It meant a lot to me. I haven't been able to face the fact that I hurt you back then. I have never been able to forgive myself for my actions toward you. I can only pray that you find it in your heart to forgive me." He reached over and took my hand. Thank you also for your support today. Having you reach out for my hand and say, 'It's OK' gave me the strength that I needed then."

"Tony," I said, "I am still trying to recover from all of this. Finally understanding what happened to us because of Robin, today meeting your parents and family, it has also taken me suddenly. I think I need time to put all of this in order, and I guess the key question for me is at the end, what do I do with it?"

"Maureen," he said, looking me straight in the face, still holding on to my hand, "I have never stopped loving you. I had lost all hope of ever having you again. Since I ran into you and all of this has transpired, I have been praying to God that he would allow you to forgive me. Maureen, I am sorry I hurt you, but maybe if I were man enough back then, I would have come to you and explained everything like my mother advised me to do, and I would have followed my heart and done what I wanted to do."

I felt the tears start to sting my eyes. I didn't want to cry; I wanted to be so much stronger, but my emotions were getting the better of me. I know this was tearing him up. It was in this face, his voice, and his body language. As I gazed into his face, his eyes that I so loved, the sadness and the hurt were quite visible. I could feel the raw emotions that came off of him. He knew how much he had hurt me, and I think that was what was killing him the most.

He reached over and pulled me into his arms, holding me tightly. My tears just ran down my cheeks. He moved his head, and his lips found mine. He kissed me so deeply, every emotion in me was unleashed, and my mind was in turmoil. I would feel the desperation in his kiss, the way he held on to me as if he was holding something so precious and was afraid of letting it get away. I broke the connection, and I stood up. He got up too.

"I am sorry, Maureen. I didn't mean to offend you."

I turned to him and held his hand. "Tony, you didn't offend me. It's just that all of this is sudden for me. There are so many emotions going through me right now that it's scary."

"I know what you mean," he agreed with me. "I love you, Maureen, always did and always will. As I said before, I am sorry." He released my hand, and with a slight smile, he said, "I better be going. It has been a long day, and a beautiful day. Thanks for coming."

"Thank you too, for a lovely day. I enjoyed myself and thank you for this moment. It means a lot to me."

I walked him to the door. He briefly hugged me, and as he turned to walk away, he asked if he could call me tomorrow. I told him yes. I close the door and return to the living room. I sat on the sofa, my mind in a whirl. *"Calm down,"* I told myself, but so many thoughts were racing through my mind.

When he kissed me, I could feel my heart pounding in my chest. In an instant, all my old feelings for him came rushing back. It was as if a dam had broken loose and sent the water rushing down to the valley below. This can't be happening to me. I don't know what to do. He said he never stopped loving me. For seven long years, this man has been tucked far away in my mind. The way he kissed me and held me, suddenly, all the anger, all the hurt, all the disappointment seemed to have been washed away in the great water surge that flooded my mind.

But I have to take all of this in stride. I cannot go running back to him because he tells me these things. I have to sort all of this out and make sure in my mind and in my heart that I want to take a chance with him again.

"I forgive you, Tony," I said the words out loud to the empty room.

"I forgive you, Robin."

Today at church, I could feel as if God was touching my being as we repeated the Lord's Prayer. I knew then that I had to forgive in order for me to be forgiven of all the mistakes I have made. I have my whole life ahead of me. I am not going to walk around day by day holding on to the past.

"Thank you, Father God, for this today and for touching my life."

I got up, and as I did, I felt as if a heavy weight had been lifted off of me. My whole being felt as light as a feather.

Chapter 13

The telephone rang, and I reached over and picked it up.

"Hello, am I forgotten?" The voice on the other end asked. It was Lisa.

She was right; I had not spoken to her in over a week, and I had not even told her about what was going on and how things have transpired between Tony and me.

"Of course not! Don't be silly! I couldn't forget you, and you wouldn't let me forget you anyhow," I said to her with a grin on my face that she could not see.

"You got that right. So, what's going on? What are you doing for Labor Day weekend?"

I hesitated for a minute, and I said, "Tony is having a family barbecue on Sunday evening, and he invited me."

I heard a gasp, followed by "Excuse me! What did you just say?" Lisa partly shouted.

"You heard me; I am going to Tony's for a barbecue."

"Whaat! Girl, what is going on?" Lisa said.

"Lisa," I asked, "what are you doing Saturday? Come over so we can talk."

"OK," she said. "What time shall I come?"

"Around three is good, I have to run an errand earlier in the day. I should be back before three. I will explain everything then."

"All right, I cannot wait to hear this. I will see you on Saturday."

"OK. Bye." I hung up the phone.

I know Lisa will be surprised to hear what has been happening between Tony and me. While Lisa was my best friend, I had not felt like discussing with her the recent developments. I am not sure why, but I wanted to hold on to all of it for a while to think on it.

Summer is coming to an end; this weekend is Labor Day, the unofficial beginning of fall. For the past week, I have spoken to Tony every day. He has called me, or I have called him. We have not talked of anything serious pertaining to us—little chat about how our day is going, Ezra, and the well-being of his family.

When I spoke to him yesterday, he told me about the barbecue and suggested that I come a little earlier so as to give me some playtime with Ezra. We agreed that I would get there about 2:00 p.m.

I was actually looking forward to playing with Ezra. This has been an interesting summer. James left in June, and I ran into Tony at the end of July. In a matter of four weeks, so much has transpired that I don't know what to make of it all. Tony coming back into my life suddenly has put me into a tailspin.

I must admit that talking to Tony has lifted my spirits. In my heart, I secretly hoped that maybe, just maybe, Tony was speaking the truth when he said he loved me and always will. Could it be possible that after seven years, he still carried this love for me even though he had no idea if I had gotten married and was somebody else's wife? Why would he hold on to a love for me?

I wondered if he was involved with anyone else since Robin passed. He's a young strong man; I am sure he yearns for companionship. How does one sift through all this to come up with a rational decision? I wondered.

Saturday afternoon, Lisa arrived as planned. I know she was dying to find out what was going on. I hadn't told her anything. There were some things and thoughts that I didn't want to share.

I filled her in on the stuff that Robin did and told her I went to church with Tony and his family last Sunday. She listened attentively and, at the end, just smiled.

"Well, my dear," she said, "that is some story. How do you feel, Maureen? Do you believe him, and will you be willing to get involved with him again?"

"I am still thinking," I replied.

"All I can say is to think really carefully before you act. This is one decision you are going to have to make yourself. I am here as a friend for you to talk to, but don't expect any advice from me. I could never relate to your feelings, so I will not advise you."

"Yeah, I know, I agree with you—that way, whatever the outcome, I have no one to blame. The decision will be mine."

"Well, actually," Lisa continued, "I will offer one piece: take your time and don't rush into anything. He has been out of your life for the past seven years. He is not the same person he was when you both were in college. He has a child he is raising, and that has to be factored in as part of your decision making. It would mean instant motherhood for you and having to look after the child of a woman who caused you a lot of grief."

As usual Lisa was listing all the critical things I have to consider.

"I believe I will be able to handle it. If you meet Ezra, you will fall in love with him too. He is so adorable. But I hear you. I definitely agree with you. This is not a decision to be made overnight. This is going to call for some serious thought and some heavy praying.

Lisa, how does something like this happen the way it did? You suggested I look for a new apartment, I go into Bed-Stuy and stop by a park, and the rest is history. What do you make of that"?

"Girl, that beats me, but I have always heard that there are no coincidences. I believe in predestination. It explains a lot of things that happens in life. When you think about this stuff, it really makes you think. What if you had stopped by the park an hour later, would you have met him, or would he have left already, or what if you didn't stop at all?

Also, what about him coming to your office as an auditor? I am sure neither one of you in your wildest dreams would have thought of that. Who knows, maybe fate has brought you two back together. The question now is, do you believe?

"Wow! Girl, this is deep, but I also believe like the song says, 'Que sera sera, whatever will be, will be.'"

"Well, it sounds like you got a plan." Lisa smiled. "Just make sure you keep me updated on this adventure. I would hate to think you are holding out on me."

"Nah, just taking quiet time to think. You know I will keep you updated."

"You better, because when this wedding comes off, I have to be up front and center. You know I will have your back. It's time I help plan a wedding."

"What wedding? Why don't you start planning your own if you want to be a wedding planner so bad?" I said to her. In the back of my mind, sometimes Lisa irks me with her smart remarks.

"At last, I would love to, but I am still looking, but if your luck is changing, maybe mine will also. Who knows, we could have a double wedding," Lisa gestured.

"Keep dreaming, you lunatic." I busted out laughing.

"You never know," she replied, "you never know." We chatted a while longer, and I walked with her to the train station. It gave me an opportunity to stop by the vegetable stand to pick up some fruits.

As I walked back home, I was thinking about Lisa. She has been a true friend to me, someone I could talk to and who always shed a different perspective on things. But like she said, the decisions I make will be all mine.

My mind shifted to the upcoming bar-b-que and I wondered who will be there? Most likely family and friends. He clearly wants me to be involved, or I could be just a friend among all the friends that he has. There I go again, overthinking everything. I am just going to go, play with Ezra, and enjoy the barbecue.

Before I knew it the week had gone by and Labor Day weekend was here. I arrived at Tony's as planned. He and Aunt Mae were busy setting things up. Tony greeted me with a hug and a kiss to my cheek. From the bottom of the stairs, he shouted, "Ezra, Miss Maureen is here."

I could hear the rush of little feet running, and he appeared at the top of the stairs. He was down the stairs in a flash, and his little arms went around me.

"Hello, Miss Maureen," he gushed, "you come to play with me?" I bent over and gave him a kiss, and before I knew it, he had taken my hand and started to lead me up the stairs.

"Easy, Ezra," said Tony, "she is coming."

"Maureen,"—Tony looked at me— "I really appreciate this. I have to finish setting up outside. When you get tired, come outside. I will let you know when the guests start arriving."

"OK," I said, "we'll have fun. I'll come down when he gets tired."

I followed a smiling Ezra up to his room, and he was so excited, he didn't know what game he wanted to play first. He had some wooden building blocks and a booklet that illustrated the various designs that could be made with the blocks. We decided to build a castle. Then he wanted to build a ramp so he could race his toy cars on it. I looked at my watch, and two hours had gone by so quickly.

As I thought of going downstairs to see how the preparations were going, Tony appeared at the door and said that some guests were here. He went into the closet and pulled out a pair of shorts and a shirt and laid them on the bed and told Ezra to get dressed so he could come downstairs. Tony took my arm and began leading me to the door.

"When you are finished dressing," he said to Ezra, "come downstairs. Miss Maureen will be downstairs while you get dressed."

"OK," he said. "Miss Maureen, I will be right down. Dad, did you see my castle? Miss Maureen said that long ago, there were castles and knights and dragons. Dad, can I get a dragon?"

"Dragons don't exist anymore," his father said, "but we will talk about it later, OK?"

"All right," he replied. We walked out the door and closed it behind us.

Tony looked at me. "He is a handful, isn't he?"

"He's a boy with a vivid imagination, and he is adorable" was my reply. Without another word, he reached over and took me in his arms, his lips slowly descended on mine, and he kissed me.

"I missed you," he said.

Before I had a chance to reply, a voice that seemed to be ascending the stairs called out, "Tony, Ezra, are you up here?"

Tony turned. "It's Mom," he said. "I am up here, Mom. I will be right down." He looked at me and smiled. "We will continue this later."

"Tony, I said, "you may want to wipe the lipstick off your lips."

"I don't want to," he replied. "OK, I will." He took a piece of paper towel from his pocket and wiped his lips before heading downstairs.

"Hi, Mom," he greeted her at the bottom of the stairs and hugged and kissed her. "You remember Maureen? She has been keeping Ezra busy while Aunt Mae and I get things set up."

"Mrs. Bradley." I approached, and she reached over to hug me.

"Maureen, lovely to see you again. Don't forget, it's Marion, please call me Marion," she said.

"Sorry, Marion, I will remember next time."

We all walked through the kitchen and down the steps leading to the yard. There were a number of people there already. We walked over to Mr.

Bradley first, who gave me a firm handshake and said he was happy to see me. Tony introduced me to people as we walked around. He had hired a DJ who had just finished setting up and started to play some music.

Shondell, his sister, came in and, as she saw me, walked over to say hello and give me a hug. Tony introduced me to his friend Ron who was manning the barbecue grill. Ezra appeared at my side, and I looked him over, and he ran off to play with two little friends who had just arrived.

Over the next several hours, we enjoyed the music, the food, and the company. We danced to the beat of reggae, soca, and calypso. The sun went down, and the yard was lit with color bulbs strung around the yard, plus the lit citronella candles to keep the mosquitoes at bay.

I met many of Tony's friends. Everyone was friendly, and I suspected one or two of them may have heard of me by the way they reacted at meeting me. Tony, for the most part, was laughing, talking, and being the perfect host. Every now and then, I would realize that he was watching me.

I too sneaked looks him as he circulated. He was wearing a light-blue polo shirt and khaki shorts. His upper body looked so defined, his chest, his arms. He wasn't bulky, just nicely sculptured. His haircut low and shaped to suit his face, his moustache neatly trimmed. He looked fine as hell. I couldn't look at him without a smile coming to my face and my heart doing its happy dance.

At eleven o'clock, Tony walked up to me and said that it was time Ezra started getting ready for bed, and he wanted to know if I wanted to read him a bedtime story.

"I know he is going to want you, and not me." Tony smiled.

"Not a problem. I will be happy to read him his story." We found Ezra, and you could see that he was looking tired. I took him by the hand, and I said, "It's time to take your bath and get ready for bed."

"No, I'm not tired. I want to play some more," he said.

"Look," I replied, "all the kids have gone home because it's late and it's their bedtime. I will read you a bedtime story, how about that?"

"OK," he said. Do you want to stay over? You could sleep in my room."

"I can't stay over, but I'll stay until you fall asleep," I told him as I touched his little chin. We went upstairs, and he took a bath. He put on his pajamas and got in the bed.

"What story would you like me to read? I see you have a lot of books."

"I don't want to read a book. Tell me more about the knights and the dragons."

"OK," I said, so at that point, I invented a story based on a combination of King Arthur and the Knights of the Round Table and all the other stories and movies I have seen about medieval times. He listened attentively.

At the end of the story, he said, "Miss Maureen, do you want to be my mommy?"

The breath caught in my throat. I was stunned. My brain started firing off questions in quick succession: *What do I say? How do you answer a kid, so he understands? Did I give this kid false hope? Did I do something wrong here by getting too close to this kid?* **I know** he must have seen the look of turmoil that covered my face as I search for the words to say.

He continued, "I know you don't look like my mommy, but that's OK. Miss Maureen, look at my mommy and me."

With that, he pulled open his nightstand drawer and pulled out a picture. It was a picture of Robin holding him; he looked as if he could have been a year old. It was a beautiful picture; Robin had a lovely smile on her face as she held her baby boy. I gazed at the picture.

"Beautiful," I said, "and who is that cutest little boy?" I asked with a big smile on my face.

"That's me," he said proudly. Suddenly, the bedroom opened, and Tony came in.

"Ready for bed, Ezra?" he asked.

"Yes, Daddy." I handed him back the picture, and he put it back to its original place. I reached over and kissed him on his forehead.

"Good night, my darling," I whispered, and I walked out the door.

"Maureen," Tony said, "wait for me outside." I closed the door and stood in the hallway. A few minutes later, Tony walked out. He walked up to me, and I went into his arms; he held me tightly.

"Maureen, I heard what Ezra asked you."

"Tony, am I doing the right things by being here? He is a child, he doesn't understand, but I would hate to disappear from his life."

"You don't have to disappear from his life or mine. Maureen, I know a lot has happened to us in the past. Do you think you could find it in your heart to give us an opportunity to see if we could make it?"

"Tony, I am so afraid to be hurt again."

"Sweetheart, believe me, this man you see before you is a different person from Tony back then. I know what I want. I am willing to work to get it, and I respect and love you enough to give you the time to make up your mind one way or the other."

"OK," I said. He pulled me back into his arms and just held me.

"Let's go back down. Guests are leaving, and I need to be there to thank them for coming."

I followed him downstairs. His mom and daddy were about ready to go, and Marion came over to say good night and reminded me of her lunch invitation. At midnight, the DJ stopped playing, and one by one, the guests eventually left. In the meantime, I had started helping Aunt Mae clean up the kitchen and pack food away in the refrigerator.

Tony said to Aunt Mae, "I know you are tired. Maureen and I will finish off. Go put your feet up."

"Best idea I have heard all day," she replied, a tired smile on her face. "I am going home and get in my bed—that way, I can sleep late tomorrow."

"When you're ready, let me know, I will walk you home," Tony told her.

"Walk me two doors away? Son, I have been in this neighborhood when you were a babe in arms. I have no fear of walking on this block. Every man, woman, child, and pet know Aunt Mae."

"Be that as it may," he replied strongly, "I am walking you home to make sure you are in your house safe. You know now crazy these kids are out here. They shot someone in the next block last week. I am not taking any chances with you. I don't want to have to hurt anybody for messing with my aunt, but I will if they mess with you."

When Aunt Mae was ready, Tony left to walk her home, and I continued with the cleanup. He was back within ten minutes; I figured he checked around and made sure everything was in order before coming back in. By 1:30 a.m., we had finished our cleanup.

"Maureen," Tony said, "I can't thank you for all that you did today. I know you must be tired also. I hate that you have to drive home by yourself and have to look for a parking. Let me drive you home. Leave your car here, and tomorrow, I will pick you up and you can get your car at that time."

"Tony, I am fine. I have come home later than this and found a parking and everything was fine."

"Maureen, I don't want anything to happen to you. I wouldn't be able to live with myself, not to mention, Ezra would not have the mommy he wants."

"Oh oh,"—I smiled— "you are too much. I know you have got to be tired also. I'll tell you what, I will drive home, I will look for a parking, and when I start my walk to my door, I will call you on the cell—that way, it would be as if you are walking with me, you will be with me every step, and you will know that I am home safe and sound."

"Are you sure, Maureen? I am not too tired to take you. You are precious to me."

"I promise," I replied. "I will be fine. I will do as I just said." He walked me to my car, and I did as I said I would, and once I was in my apartment and locked the door behind me, I told him good night.

"Good night, darling," he said. "I will call you later in the day. Thanks for everything. You're the best." We hung up, and I went to bed, tired but happy.

Chapter 14

"Hello, Maureen, it's Marion," the voice on the other end of the phone said.

"Hello, Marion," I replied. "How are you?"

"I am fine. I am calling to see if you are available for lunch next Saturday?"

"Sure, I don't have anything that I am committed to. What time should I come?"

"Let's say around 1:00 p.m. Is that OK?"

"Yes, that's OK. Tony has volunteered to bring you over on his way to the church. Is that OK also?"

"Sure, it's all right," I replied. I could just imagine the two of them talking about this, and I am sure Tony eagerly raised his hand to do this.

"He will let you know what time he would you pick up. I am looking forward to seeing you. Thank you, my dear."

"Thank you also. I will see you on Saturday." I hung up the phone.

The last couple of weeks have been interesting to say the least. It had been two weeks since Tony's barbecue. I have not seen him since that time, but I have talked to him every day since then. He had even begun texting me little messages.

Sometimes at lunchtime, he would text to say, "Enjoy your lunch"; or as I am leaving work, "Travel safely"; or at night, he would text and say, "Good night sweetheart xxxx oooo." I have to admit, I have been thinking about a possibility of an us.

Some days I feel optimistic; on other days, fear and hurt raise their ugly heads and send me into uncertainty. Ezra's question to me still resonates in my ears. It was the sweetest thing and the most fearful at the same time. I have grown so close to him in the short space of time that I first played with him. I question myself if my feelings are out of a sense of pity for him not having a mother, or did I truly care about him? He had no way of knowing how close I had been to being his mother. To a child, the world is so simple; but to us, we do a great job of gumming it up.

I am so afraid to take a chance; I couldn't bear another breakup and especially a second breakup with Tony. I would feel like a total idiot if that were to happen to me.

Friday evening, Tony called to say that he would pick me up at twelve thirty to drop me off at his mom's house. He had a meeting with the men's ministry at the church and would pick me up at the end of the meeting.

"Maureen, I hope you didn't mind me telling Mom I'll pick you up," he said as we talked.

"No, I don't see anything wrong with that, as long as it's on your way and I am not taking you out of your way to do this."

"You know something? Even if I had to go out of my way, I would do it for you."

"Why is that?" I asked.

"Because, Miss. Maureen, I'll do anything for you."

"Oh really, when did all of this start?"

"A long time ago, and it remains the same to this day."

"If you say so," I chuckled.

"Oh, but I do, I do," he replied, chuckling along with me. We ended the conversation with my sending a kiss for Ezra and a promise that I will be ready when he arrives.

As planned, Tony picked me up and dropped me off at his mom's. He came out the car with me and walked me up the steps to Marion, who was standing at the open door. He had called ahead as we turned onto the street and told Mom to come to the front door. He kissed me on the cheek as he left and said he should be back by three. Marion also hugged me and welcomed me to her home.

The Bradley's home was on Howard Avenue and Sutter Avenue; you could actually walk to the church from their house. It would be a nice walk during spring, summer, and early fall. Winter, however, I think it would be a bit much to attempt it in the cold. The living room and dining room were beautifully decorated. Pictures of the children during their school days filled the walls, along with certificates, plaques, and awards given to the family for various activities. Marion had the dining room table set up for lunch.

"Marion, I brought some wine, I hope that's OK?"

"Perfect, we can have a glass with our lunch."

For lunch, she had prepared salmon with garlic sauce, her specialty, she said, served with wild rice and smothered cabbage. It was quite delicious.

During lunch, the conversation started off with Ezra and how much he talks about me. Then she asked questions about my career and my organization. Apparently, she had heard about us and thought we were doing a wonderful job with the housing situation in Brooklyn.

"You know," Marion said, "this housing problem is something I have mixed emotions about. On one hand, I see when people pay their rent and are not given adequate services, and then on the other hand, I know of people who at the slightest problem refuse to pay their rent, and that puts the homeowner, especially small homeowners, in trouble with their bills."

"I know. That's a problem that we face. Many times, we have had to say to clients that they should continue paying and they could take the landlord to court. Some agree, and others don't. I tried to explain that by arbitrarily withholding rent, they are taking the law into their own hands and not letting the court make a decision."

"It seems like you love your job!"

"I really do. I remember when I was little, we lived in a building without heat and hot water for a whole winter. I remembered that we slept in the living room—my mother, father, and baby brother on the sofa pullout bed, and I in the love seat. We burned the oven in the kitchen all night to help provide us with heat. I wondered if, at that time, my parents were aware of how dangerous a situation that was. We could have all been poisoned by carbon monoxide. I don't believe I will ever forget that experience.

I am proud to be part of an organization that is dedicated to fighting for proper and safe housing for all New Yorkers. I would never want a child to live that experience that I had."

"That is an excellent example of how our life experiences motivate us to fight for change, instead of sitting back and hoping someone else does something about it. I admire your courage."

We finished lunch, and I helped clear away the dishes. She washed our dishes and put them to drain, and we walked into the living room where we continued our chat. I took the opportunity to look at the school pictures of Tony and his sisters through the years.

"Maureen," Marion said as we sat talking, "I am so glad to have finally met you. That day when Tony went to your job and saw you, he told me he was so shocked. It took all of his willpower to stand his ground, and he couldn't believe it. He felt as if God had finally heard him and was answering his prayers. I told him to never stop praying. He knows that God's time is not our time, and it is for us to be patient and wait and murmur not.

You know, what happened to Tony broke my heart. As a mother, I had never felt so helpless. I was so angry at that girl for what she did. I know I shouldn't refer to her like that, but I never saw her as a daughter-in-law. She almost destroyed this family. Joe and I always made it a point to show a united front when it came to the children. We upheld each other with whatever decisions were made. When this thing happened to Tony, I didn't agree with Joe telling him to marry Robin. We had some heated arguments on it—yes, I understood his argument about how the congregation may view this, but to force Tony to marry her after she tricked and drugged him was too much to bear. I cried many days when it first occurred. I couldn't bear to see my son so broken up. He told me he loved you and he wanted to marry you. I told him to go to you and explain what had happened. He said he would, but later, he told me he was too ashamed to face you. He felt like it was his fault. He kept saying if only he didn't go into the apartment, if only he had not drunk the punch. He was devastated. I had to talk with him and pray with him to comfort him."

I sat there and just listened; it was so heartbreaking. I wondered if people, as they plot and plan, have any idea what rippling affects their selfish plans have on others.

"Then if that wasn't bad enough," Marion continued, after they got married, she told Tony she wanted to move to Georgia, as her family had a place they could use. I believe that was her excuse to get him away from around his family so she could be in total control. After they moved, we saw Tony one time when he came up for his uncle's funeral. Anytime we could suggest that we could visit, he always found an excuse for us not to come. I believe she did not want us around, and he did not want us to know the condition he was living under. Maureen, I want to tell you that I never ceased praying for my son. I prayed that God will deliver him. I was shocked when he called us to say Robin was dying. I couldn't believe it."

"Marion, I don't know what to say. I thought that Tony had been secretly seeing Robin behind my back and had ended up getting her pregnant. I too was in a state of shock when Tony broke up with me, and the next thing I heard, he had married Robin. I couldn't believe it."

"I know that had to be the worst thing for you to have been through. If Tony had done what I told him to do, at least you have had a better understanding of what took place.

What happened to Tony, I wouldn't wish it on anybody's child, but he is a strong man, and he has been able to come through this stronger than he went in. He has Ezra who adores him and looks up to him, and I think that's what keeps him going."

I heard the lock on the door turned, and in walked Tony and Mr. Bradley. A quick glance to my watch, and I saw it was 3:30 p.m.

"Hello, we are home," Tony announced as he made his way to the living room. "We are hungry. I hope you left lunch for us."

"Nope, we ate it all. This was women's lunch day." She smiled. "Just kidding, there's food for the two men in my life." With that, she got up, excused herself, and headed off to the kitchen. So, this is where Tony got his sense of humor—from Mom.

Mr. Bradley walked in, walked up to me, and shook my hand. "Hello, Maureen. Nice to see you again."

"Likewise, Pastor Bradley," I responded with a smile. He turned and followed his wife into the kitchen.

"Hi, babe," Tony said. Has Mom been talking your ears off?"

"We have been chatting. How was your meeting?"

"Very good. We are starting a counseling ministry aimed at young men. We want to reach out to those men in their twenties and thirties who may be having problems with relationships. We also want to help with finding jobs and referrals for training opportunities."

"Sounds like something that is much needed," I responded to him. "This financial crisis is really hitting us hard. So many people have lost jobs, and nothing creates more problems in a relationship than finance."

"Did you enjoy your lunch?" he asked.

"Yes, everything was great."

At this point, Marion called to Tony that lunch was ready. I expected he would have walked away and go into the dining room to eat. To my surprise, he reached out and held on to my hands and raised me out of my chair. As I got up, his arms went around my waist, giving me a hug. "Come and sit with me while I eat."

He held my hand, and we walked into the dining room. Pastor Bradley was already seated before his plate, and Tony took his seat. Pastor Bradley blessed the food, and they began eating. Marion, in the meantime, left and reappeared with two small plates that held a slice of chocolate cake each.

"Maureen, I was so caught up in our conversation, I forget to serve dessert. Ah well, it's OK, we'll have it now while they have their lunch."

For the next half an hour, we sat and talked. After their meal, the men had their dessert, and we finished the bottle of wine that I brought. I felt very comfortable sitting there, eating, and talking. Marion had made me feel welcome from the very beginning, and I grew more comfortable as the afternoon wore on.

The next time I checked my watch, it was 5:00 p.m., and Tony said it was time he got going. Ezra had gone to play with a friend but should be getting home right about now.

"Marion," I said as I prepared to leave, "I had a wonderful afternoon. Thank you for inviting me."

"Maureen, I enjoyed every minute of it. You must come again another afternoon. It would most likely be after we return from our trip, but I will call you. Now that I have your number, we will keep in touch. That is all right with you, I hope?"

"Of course, please feel free to call me anytime. I will give you a call also."

"Great, I am looking forward to us talking."

We hugged each other, and I left.

Tony dropped me off and, with a quick kiss to my cheek, said that he would call me later. I thanked him for taking me, and I walked into my apartment.

As I sat reliving the afternoon, my mind went to Robin. I know I said I forgive her, but she deserved to have her ass kicked. I know I shouldn't be thinking this way—after all, the woman is dead, but she did some serious damage to a lot of people.

How in hell did she become so obsessed and crazy about Tony? Marion said she told Tony to let me know what went on. Who knows what inspired him to not tell me? If he did at that time, who's to say how I would have reacted? I don't think I would have taken it lightly, especially if I knew she planned it. I would have confronted her, and if she had gotten in my face, it would not have been pretty. I shuddered to think how I would have gone postal on her ass.

Who knows, my actions back then may have had a negative effect on my life, but as the saying goes, "All's well that ends well."

All of this is in the past, and I will let it remain there. Makes no sense at this point thinking about what I could or should have done.

My thoughts shifted to the loving feelings that are growing inside me toward Tony. It is quite clear that his parents seem to have regards for me, and of course there is Ezra, my favorite of all. For so long, I had wanted a child—looks like without even giving birth, I have a baby boy, Ezra.

Chapter 15

Fall was here; the leaves had turned to all the lovely colors of fall, and now they were falling. I was sad to see summer go; even on the hottest days, in spite of how sticky and uncomfortable it got, I love summer. Everything is just so much brighter in summer; the days are longer as the sun sets so much later in the evening. Soon, the holidays will be upon us, and with that comes the winter and the cold days and nights.

Tony and I were becoming closer. I was trying my best not to get too involved; I had heard what Tony had to say, and it was pretty much confirmed by the conversation I had with his mom, but I was still hesitant. I knew that this was something I had to think very carefully on; it was a decision that was not to be made emotionally.

For the past couple of weeks, we continued our daily talks; I also met him for lunch on two occasions. On those occasions he was downtown Brooklyn performing an audit, and he took the opportunity to invite me for lunch.

He had been true to his words so far when he said that he was willing to give me the time to make up my mind one way or the other, as to whether I was prepared to give a relationship with him a try.

During our get-together, we talked about our jobs and the latest happenings, and shared moments of laughter. I believe we have been discovering little things about each other that we have developed over the years since we have been apart.

He tells me he likes to cook, and he makes a mean fish stew. I told him that I too love to cook also, and we promised that one day, we'll have a cook-off with each of us cooking our signature dishes.

"Of course, he said, "we will have to invite some friends to sample these dishes and give us their opinion."

"Sounds like a plan. Name your date and let the battle of the cooks begin."

We both burst out laughing; it's these little things that I find so endearing, a sense of humor that brightens all the dark corners.

Tony had given me a standing invite to church and told me any Sunday I wanted to go, just let him know and he would pick me up.

That Friday, as we sat having lunch, I told him I would like to go to church this Sunday. He smiled and told me he would pick me at 10:30 a.m. I also asked him if he would like to stay for lunch after church. An even bigger smile covered his face.

"I would love to come to lunch. Who's cooking by the way?" He said it with a straight face.

"Oh, you're funny! This will be an opportunity for you to see what your competitor has up her sleeve."

"I'm not afraid. I am ready to meet the challenge."

"OK, don't say I didn't warn you."

"By the way, isn't your birthday coming up in the next couple of weeks?" Tony inquired.

"You remembered? Yes, it's November 5."

"Do you have any plans on how you will celebrate it?"

"I haven't given it much thought. It's a Thursday, so chances are I will be working."

"I would love to take you out for a night on the town, but it would have to be Saturday, would you mind? It will be a couple of days after the birthday, but there is nothing that says we can't celebrate over a number of days."

"I don't mind. The weekend is better—that way we don't have to watch the clock because we have to go to work the next day."

"So let me do this properly. Maureen, I would be honored if you will allow me to take you out for your birthday on Saturday, November 7, shall we say 7:00 p.m."

"Tony, you are too much! Yes, I would be happy to spend the evening with you. On that note," I said, "I have to start heading back to the office. I enjoyed my lunch and the company."

"Gee, time sure flies when you're having fun. I too have to get back also. My partner, you remember Ralph, Mr. King, he is like my father, strict, but he's a good guy."

He took care of the tab, and we exited the restaurant. We touched lips briefly, and we went in separate directions back to our offices.

As I walked along, I was thinking, looks like I will be seeing a lot of Tony—church and lunch on Sunday and dinner for my birthday. I like the fact that I don't feel pressured to make a decision. We have been talking, meeting for lunch, and it has been so pleasant.

Tony has been a gentleman, a hug, a kiss to the cheek, a touch to the lips, no groping or trying to get in my panties, just great. I felt as if we were two people who met and started seeing each other to see if there was any chemistry between them. It felt as if it could be a new beginning and I wanted to take my time.

Sunday came, and we went to church. Of course, Ezra was there with Aunt Mae. He gets there a little earlier as Sunday school for the kids begins at ten. He was all smiles to see me and, as usual, wanted to know if I will come by to play later. I told him not today, but I will come another day.

Church was wonderful; the service was done by Assistant Pastor Henry, as Pastor Bradley and Marion were on their trip to Israel. At the end of the service, I kissed Ezra and promised him I will be coming by soon.

For lunch, I served shrimps sauteed with tomatoes, onions and ginger on a bed of white rice, honey baby carrots, and a tossed salad.

Tony had removed his jacket and tie, and I had changed into a halter-top sundress. I opened a bottle of white wine, and we sat down to lunch. Tony said grace, and we toasted our first meal in my home.

"I can see where this competition is going to be tough," he said as he enjoyed his lunch.

"I got nothing to say," I replied. "I will just do my thing."

"And it looks as if you know what you're doing. I am scared of you," he said between chewing and a chuckle.

We ate our meal while we talked about the service, college days, and us. I felt to myself that with every encounter I had with Tony, I would feel my heart softening and that old familiar feelings that I had for him beginning to come back stronger.

After lunch we retired to the living room, and I put on a jazz CD. I remembered him telling me that he loves jazz. I am not a die-hard jazz fan, but there are some jazz songs that I like. I heard this vendor on Fulton Street playing the CD one day as I was walking by. I liked what I heard, so I bought it. Around the third track, Tony said,

"Where did you get that CD? That right there is my jam." With that, he reached over and pulled me up and started to dance with me.

"What, you just break in to dance at the drop of a hat?" I said, smiling, his arms around my waist, and he was humming along to the song.

"I can't talk while I am dancing. I have to concentrate on my steps."

With that, he whirled me around and brought me back to face him and continued to dance to the end of the song.

"I must say you dance very well, for an old lady," he said, still holding me tightly around my waist.

"Funny, I was saying the same thing about you, old man."

"Oh no, you didn't." He laughed out loudly. "Touché."

With that, he lifted me up and sprung around, slowly lowering me back to the floor. He encircled my face with his hand and kissed me; first, lightly, but as my lips parted, the kiss deepened, and I could feel the electricity start to spark within us. His hand left my face and traveled down my arms to my back before encircling my waist, pulling me closer and tighter to him.

At last, he released me, and we stood there looking at each other, his eyes searching my face. *What was he looking for? I wondered. Maybe a look of love? Desire?* I smiled, and I sat down on the sofa. He came and sat beside me and took my hands.

"I hope I didn't scare you just now," he said.

"No, I love it, sort of reminded me of the Tony back in college, impetuous. It was one of the things I loved about you. Or should I say love about you."

"Maureen, I look at you, and my heart starts to sing. I touch you, and I never want to let you go. Every fiber of my being loves you and wants you. Every day, I pray that we could start a life together. I feel as if I have lost so much time that should have been with you, and I won't want to lose anymore."

"Tony, I have been thinking about us, and I am a little afraid, but I have decided that I want to give us a chance."

"You mean it, Maureen? Oh, baby, I love you. As God is my witness, Maureen, I am here to stay. I have loved you from the beginning. I made a mistake that almost cost me my life and happiness, but God is giving me a second chance, and I thank him, I thank you, and I am going to treasure and protect this with my life if need be."

He pulled me into his arms and held on to me tightly.

"Maureen, it has been a lovely afternoon. I am so happy right now; I am not sure if my feet are on the ground. I am going to leave now because I don't trust myself around you at this point. I have to take it slow, but looking at you, hearing what you just said, the man in me wants you so badly, but I want to wait for the right time. Thank you for lunch. Thank you for being the awesome woman that you are."

He kissed me lightly on the lips and put on his jacket. He pushed the tie in this pocket and, holding my hand, started toward the door. I walked with him to the front door, one final hug, and he left. I close the door and return to my apartment.

I sat on the sofa. "Well, Maureen," I said to myself, "you did it. I hope you are ready for this because it looks like there is no turning back."

"Father God," I said, "I feel you touching my life. Give Tony and me the strength and courage to make it this time."

My respect for Tony went higher when I heard him say how he felt. He knew that, at this stage, this was not the time to try to get me in bed, in spite of how he felt, but I was flattered by his raw admission of desire for me, and I understood it. He is a healthy young man, and the woman that he loves just told him she was ready to take a chance with him, something that he has been praying for. In my heart, I felt like I was doing the right thing. I am going to give love one more try and pray that it does not hurt me again.

Chapter 16

"I have decided to start seeing Tony again," I said to Lisa as we sat across the table from each other, eating lunch.

"Somehow I am not surprised," she replied with a half-crooked smile. "It's hard to break the bonds of first love and true love. That first day, when you told me Tony was back and your insides felt like jelly, I knew you still love that man."

"I told you that I had lunch with his mother, didn't I?"

"No, you didn't tell me that. A lot seems to have been going on that you have not been saying."

"Somewhat, I have been analyzing and praying and wanting to make a decision, and as you said before, this has to be my decision alone."

"So, what happened when you went to lunch?"

His mom is such a lovely person. She knew about the whole situation from the beginning, and she told me that she had advised Tony to tell me what was going on. She said that he was too ashamed and that he blamed himself for what happened.

I'll tell you this much, Robin really put a hurting on Tony and his family. His mother said that she went against the father because she didn't agree with him in telling Tony he had to marry Robin. Then she said that Robin tried to isolate Tony from his family by having them move to Georgia, and every time they wanted to visit, he found an excuse for them not to come. As I talked with her, I would see that it had affected her deeply. It was painful listening to her recollect what went on."

"That Robin was one wicked b—tch. I wouldn't say the word out of respect for the dead. How do people do shit like that? Well, girl, believe me when I tell you that I wish you all the best. You have been through a lot, and I am praying for you too that it will all work out."

"I haven't even told you the best part of all—Ezra asked me to be his mommy," I said with smile.

"OMG, Maureen, OMG, that has got to be the sweetest thing, but also the scariest. He loves you apparently. Isn't that ironic how this is working out? Robin's child loves you and wants you to be his mommy. Girl, God is blessing you."

"I was so taken aback when he asked me. I am sure when he is at school and other kids talk about their mommies, he doesn't have one, and maybe he wants to know what it feels like to have a mommy."

"That's possible too, but I believe because of the way you interacted with him and played with him, all of that helped form an attachment. By the way, what are you doing for your birthday?"

"Tony is taking me out to dinner."

"I should have seen that coming. Like I said, I am happy for you. I know we're at lunch and on the job, but, girl, let us have a glass of wine to celebrate. I don't think one glass will make us drunk. I feel like celebrating. I have good vibes about this."

"Lisa, you are such a crazy ass woman, I swear, I don't know what I am going to do with you."

"Girl, chill, let's drink our wine and celebrate a new beginning. Then we can go back and do the people's work."

We both burst out laughing, which bought us a few stares from nearby guests in the restaurant.

We had our glass of wine, finished our lunch, gave each other a big hug, and hurried back to work.

Lisa is so crazy, but I always enjoy talking to her, and she has proven to be such a good friend. You know you have a friend when they are honest with you and tell you what needs to be said, not what you want to hear.

I have told Lisa what is going on, how I have to bring my mom up to date.

Since the last time I had my talk with her, I have not told her much, except to let her know that I had accepted Tony's invitation to church. That was weeks ago, and since then, so much has transpired, but more importantly, I wanted her to know that I had decided to start seeing Tony again.

I finished my day at the office, and as I decided, when I got home after a light dinner, I called Mom to fill her in.

As always, she listened and said that she had confidence in me, that she knew I had thought about it long and hard to make a decision. I told her that Tony was taking me out for my birthday, and I will keep her posted. I hung up the phone from her, and I felt positive about our conversation and about the decision I had made.

With my birthday approaching, and this dinner date, I started thinking of what to wear. It was a special occasion, a new beginning, a new year of life for me, and a fresh start for Tony and me. As I sat on the edge of my bed, thinking, the phone rang. I picked it up; it was Tony.

"Hi, baby," he cooed over the line. "How are you this evening?"

"I'm fine."

"I know that right," he said, "finest thing I ever saw."

"Oh, Tony, you so bad."

"You haven't seen bad yet. I am patiently waiting until you are all mine, then you are going to see bad. This man is going to love you silly."

"Oh! Oh! I am scared of you."

"Don't be, babe. You're going to love it as much as I do. By the way, do you have any preference for a restaurant for your birthday? Is there any particular cuisine you prefer?"

"I love Thai food, but why don't you surprise me? Whatever you pick will be fine."

"OK, just dress pretty, not that you don't always, but I am taking you somewhere fancy. I want to celebrate your birthday and our new beginning."

"OK, I will be dressed with bells on."

"What, and no whistles?" He laughed out. "You got to do it right."

"OK, Mr. Tony, I'll hook it up. How is my baby Ezra?" I continued.

"He's good. I just finished helping him with homework. He is watching a show, and at the end of it, off to bed he goes."

"Kiss him good night for me. Tell him I'll see him soon."

"Will do, but don't I get a kiss too?"

"If you're good, you may," I responded with a small giggle.

"I promise I'll be good. Good night, baby. Let me go check on Ezra, and we will talk tomorrow."

"Good night, baby," I said. "Kiss, kiss."

"Thanks. Good night." He hung up.

I let out a big sigh. *"He is so adorable,"* I found myself saying out loud. Is this real? Is it really happening? Six months ago, my life was so different. Now I have a man that acts like he cares, and I have a kid that wants me to be his mother.

He wants to take me somewhere fancy. I really have to decide on what I am wearing. I have to call my hairdresser to get my hair done, and I have to get to the nail salon. I have a week to get it together before the big day. I know that somewhere in the back of my mind, there was still some apprehension. Fear still wants to rear its ugly head and put me in to doubt. I have heard it all, I have seen the way Tony acts, and I have my gut instincts, and everything says, "Grab it, Maureen. Take hold of your destiny and go for it." I have listened, and here I am.

My mind shifted to James, and I wondered how he was doing. I haven't spoken to him within the last three months. As I thought about him, I realized that sometimes we know within ourselves that a relationship is over, but we want so much to hold on. We look for every excuse to justify what is happening. We blame ourselves, believing that if you had done things differently, or if maybe you were more loving, or better in bed, all those ifs and maybes. The truth is however, when it's over, it's over, we have to be strong and let go.

All we are doing is stopping what may be waiting for us. The very thing that we want, we are blocking from coming into our lives.

When he told me he didn't want to get married and that he was leaving, it felt like a kick in the stomach; I hurt for many days. I had put so much hope and love into the relationship that I couldn't imagine that it wouldn't have worked. I have come to realize like the Tina Turner song says, "What's love got to do with it?" because it takes more than love to make a relationship work. Yes, it's important to have love and give love, but it starts with a level of respect, caring, and commitment, for each other, that makes love grow. I hope that everything was working out for him, and I really do wish him well. For me now, he is just a memory. I thank God that I had the courage to let go and allow him to send a renewal into my life.

Chapter 17

I opened my eyes. It was raining. I guess I am having a rainy birthday. I was up before the alarm went off, and I lay there thinking. Twenty-nine years old today. Over the past couple of years, I have had my ups and my downs; but when I think of my life, I feel blessed.

As I got dress for work. I review in my mind my plans for the coming week.

Next Monday, I will begin a one-week vacation. Tomorrow I was taking a personal day off, as I wanted to have my hair done so it would be fresh for Saturday.

As I walked into the kitchen, the phone rang interrupting me out of my thoughts. It was Tony.

"Happy birthday, darling. Good morning. How are you?"

"Thank you. I am doing great, feeling blessed to wake up this morning."

"I have to have a talk with Mr. Sun. He should have been on the job for my baby's birthday this morning. I wanted your day to be bright and beautiful."

"Who says it's not bright and beautiful? You called, and the room lit up."

"Ah, baby, all that sweet talk, you're going to make my head bigger." He laughed. "Anyway, baby, enjoy your day, I have to get myself together and get out of here also. Talk to you later in the day. Love you. Have a great birthday."

"Thank you. Bye. Talk to you later."

I hung up the phone. That was my first call for the day to wish me happy birthday. I am sure as the day wore on, all the calls will be coming in.

Tony made sure he was the first to call; that was so sweet of him. He has said he loves me several times since we started over, but I have not had the courage to say it back to him. So much of my old feelings have returned for him, and I know within my heart I love him, but I was not ready to say it to him yet.

I went off to work through the rain and, once on the job, I worked on tidying up my desk. I wanted to making sure that Steven would be aware of any outstanding projects that may need his attention when I am gone.

During the course of the morning, I got birthday wishes from Steven and other staff members. Lisa and my mom also called. Just before lunch, Keisha buzzed me to say that I had a delivery up front. I walked out to the reception area, and a deliveryman stood there with a huge bouquet of white, red, and yellow roses, along with two balloons.

"Ms. Coleman?" he asked.

I answered yes. He handed me the bouquet.

"Thank you. Wait a minute while I get you a tip."

"That wouldn't be necessary, ma'am. Everything is taken care of." He smiled and walked out the door.

Once in my office, I opened the wrapping and removed the card. It read "Happy birthday to the most awesome woman. Love forever, Tony."

The bouquet was beautiful. The roses mixed with the baby's breath and the fern.

This man is unbelievable; he sure is showing that he cares. I picked up the phone and called him. He answered.

"Tony, they are beautiful."

"They are a pale second to you, my darling. You like them?"

"I love them. Thank you so much. You are making my day so special."

"That's my job, anything for my baby. Enjoy them, and we'll talk later."

He hung up. I know he was on the job, and probably conditions didn't permit him to speak freely. Nevertheless, I was happy that he did all this for me.

Work was over. I made it home with the bouquet and the balloons on the train. They made my living room come alive, and I let the balloons rise to the ceiling. As I sat and watched them rise to the ceiling, I felt so lifted myself. It has been a wonderful day.

By day's end, I had received calls from my father, my brother, Diane, and Marion. I was especially happy to hear Marion, and we promised to talk so she could tell me all about the trip. She said that it was a trip that everyone should take if they could. Tony called shortly after I arrived and put Ezra on the phone to wish me a happy birthday.

"Miss Maureen, happy birthday. I made you a card for your birthday. When are you coming to get it?"

"I will check with Daddy and see if I could get it on Sunday, is that OK?"

"OK, I will ask Daddy too. Bye. Happy birthday."

He got off the phone, and Tony and I spoke for a minute.

"Let's see how you feel on Sunday," Tony said. "You could probably come over after church."

"OK, we'll see how it goes." We hung up.

I decided to go to bed early, as tomorrow was a nonstop day for me with hairdresser appointment and the nail salon, and I still wanted to find a pair of heels to go with my outfit. I had decided on a black slim-fitted dress, with a V-neck trimmed with a silver metallic-like trimming. The sleeves were wide and flared and trimmed like the neck. I wanted a pair of silver shoes to complete my look.

Before I knew Saturday was here. As I scurried around the apartment putting the finishing touches to my makeup, Tony called to say he was on his way. Knowing him he was going to be on time. By the time the doorbell rang, I had only to pick up my evening bag, and I was ready for the night. I opened the door, and he stood for a minute looking at me, admiration written all over his face.

"You look fabulous, baby," as he gave me a quick hug.

He was dressed in gray suit, light-blue pinstriped shirt with a gray-and-pink designed tie and gray shoes. He thought I look fabulous—did he look in the mirror? He looked awesome, straight off the page of a fashion magazine.

"We have to hurry he said We have reservations for 8:00 p.m. The restaurant is downtown, and with traffic and finding a park we are cutting it close. Hopefully, we will make it."

We arrived at the restaurant a couple of minutes before eight. As we walked up to the hostess, Tony gave her his name and said we had reservations for eight. We were told that our table wouldn't be ready in a few minutes and were invited to have a drink at the bar.

I had never been to this restaurant, but I have heard of it. It was right down by the water. You could see the Brooklyn and Manhattan bridges, and the lights of the Manhattan skyline. A view like this makes you fall in love with the city all over again—the view was breathtaking.

"Tony, this place is beautiful," I said, smiling from ear to ear.

"Do you want to get a drink while we wait for the table?" He asked

"I think I will wait until we are seated."

At that point, the hostess said our table was ready and had us escorted. We went past the main dining room, and I wondered where we could be seated. We approached a closed door, and our escort opened it.

Tony held on to my hand as the door opened. All I heard was "Surprise!"

I was shocked. There was a room full of people yelling "surprise." I turned to Tony.

"OMG, how did you do this?"

He held on to my hand and walked me into the center of the cheering group. They all started to sing "Happy Birthday to you." We walked to our table, which was set up at the top of the room with all the other tables to the side of it. There was a DJ, and Tony walked over to him, taking the mike, and said,

"Good evening, everyone. I want to thank you for being here this evening. I also want to thank you for keeping this a secret. Maureen had no clue what was going on." They all giggled. "Now, please take your seats and let us enjoy Maureen's birthday party. The floor is open for dancing, so please enjoy yourselves." He put down the mike and returned to my side.

"Tony, this is incredible, I can't believe it."

"I told you that this was a special day for you and for us. Let's walk around and meet your guests." With that, he held on to my hand, and we went to each table. I couldn't believe it: Mom, Dad, and my brother and his girlfriend; Marion and Pastor Bradley; Tony's two sisters and their significant others; Lisa (when I saw her, she hugged me; I was so happy); Diane and Joe; Steve and Gloria, along with other friends of Tony and of his family; and Mr. King and other coworkers of Tony. In all, there were at least forty people there.

For the next two hours, we were served dinner, and there was an open bar. I received envelops and gifts. I could hardly eat my dinner; I was so excited by all that transpired, I was beside myself. As we were served dessert, Tony went back over to the microphone.

"Hello, everyone, again. I hope that you have enjoyed your meal. I know I have. Tonight, is a special night for Maureen, and again, I want to thank all of you for coming out and making this evening special for her, for us."

He turned to face me, and he said, "Maureen, I have something important to say to you, but, first, my friend Ron is going to sing for us."

Ron walked over and took the mike and started singing. The room was hushed; you could have heard a pin drop. He sang Kelly Clarkson's "A Moment Like This." As the song ended, Ron walked the mike over to Tony and held it. The next thing I saw was Tony on his knee, and with Ron holding the mike, he said,

"Maureen, I have waited for what has seemed like a lifetime for this moment. Maureen, will you be my wife?" With that, he took the ring out of his pocket and held it up to me.

I could feel my heart thumping out of control, and tears started to sting my eyes amid the huge smile that was covering my face. I could hear friends clapping and cheering, and it all felt like I was in this dream, this twilight existence. I held out my ring finger, and he put the ring on it. "I love you, baby," he said, and he stood up, took me in his arms, and kissed me as the DJ played a song for us to dance.

We started to dance, and I heard the DJ say, "Come all you with partners, join the happy couple on the floor and help them celebrate this beautiful occasion." One by one, couples joined us, and we danced until the song ended.

When I got back to my table, Mom and Dad walked over to me. They both hugged me. Mom gave Tony a hug, and Dad shook his hand.

Mom whispered to me, "I love you, darling. We have to talk." I received so many hugs and best wishes that by the time the party finished at twelve, I wasn't sure if I was walking or being carried on a cloud. Tony drove me home and came inside.

As soon as we got inside the apartment and I closed the door, he pulled me to him.

"Girl, you looked so beautiful tonight. Maureen, are you happy?"

"Ecstatic is more like it. Tony, I still don't know how you were able to pull this off and no one said a word to me."

"I swore them to secrecy. I really wanted this night to be something you wouldn't forget. Do you feel I am rushing you by proposing to you? I know it's just about three months since that day we met in the park, but to me, I have known you for years. If things had gone the way I had it planned, we will be an old married couple by now with a couple of children. I called Steven and told him what I planned, and he gave me your mom's number, and I called her and told her and asked her to help me. Once she said she would, I got my mum in on it, and the rest is history."

"It a good thing I have a strong heart. I thought we were just going to have a quiet dinner. You blew me away with this. Tony, I am so happy. I don't believe I answered you tonight when you asked if I would be your wife. Yes, Tony, I will be honored to be your wife."

"Sweetheart," he said, "I want you to set the date whenever you are ready. I am not rushing you, but I want you to know that I am serious and you have two men waiting on you. One wants you to be his mommy and one wants you to be his wife. What can I say, you got it going on."

"Right now, I have to get back to earth before I can start to think of a date, but we will discuss it. There is so much to do to plan a wedding. I have to think it through."

"You know," he said, "I was hoping that I didn't give it away by the flowers I sent you."

"How so?"

"Well, I was told that the color of a roses has a meaning. Red is for love, yellow is for friendship, and white is a proposal of marriage."

"Really? I had never heard that. I did wonder about the three different colors, but they looked so beautiful, I thought that was all there was to it."

"It was my message to you: I love you, I want us to be best friends, and I want to marry you. Sweetheart, I am going to leave. I'll pick you tomorrow so you can get your card from Ezra."

"Are you going to church tomorrow?" I asked him.

"Yes, I try to be there every Sunday."

"Pick me up for church. I need to give God thanks for all that he is doing for me."

"Great. I'll pick you at 10:30 a.m."

"Good night, sweetheart." He held me close, kissing my face, my eyes, and ran his tongue along my eyelashes and finally my lips. His lips on mine, so sweet, I could feel my breasts start to react. I moved my body against his, and a groan escaped his lips.

"I have to go," he said. "I don't want to spoil everything by letting my manly desires take hold of me. Maureen, I want you so badly, but I am afraid that you may think that I am looking for sex, and I don't know if you are ready for that step. I have been thinking of letting us wait until we get married. We should have waited back then, but we are more mature now. What do you think about it? Don't answer now. Let's talk about it when my body isn't on fire."

"OK," I agreed.

I walked with him to the door, one last kiss, and he left. I told him to call or text me when he got home so that I would know that he was in safely.

By the time I had finished taking my clothes off and cleaning the makeup off my face, he texted to say he was home and wished me a good night. I said good night also and inserted a smiley face.

I got in the bed. I lay there for a minute, and then my attention turned to my ring. I hadn't really looked at it closely. It looked beautiful on my finger. It was a pear-shaped diamond set in white gold; it could also be platinum? I couldn't tell for sure.

My mind started to relive the evening, like the song said, some people wait a lifetime for a moment like the one Tony gave to me today. I couldn't help smiling. "Father God," I whispered, "thank you. I am so happy." I closed my eyes, and I could feel the tiredness descend on me like a ton of brick, and before long, I was fast asleep.

Chapter 18

I awoke to the ringing of the phone. I was sleeping so deeply, I barely heard it. I turned over in bed and reached over to the night table to pick up the phone.

"Hello," I said drowsily.

"Maureen, are you still sleeping? It's 9:00 a.m. I thought you would be up."

"Hi, Mum, I didn't realize it was so late. I have to get up and get ready. Tony is picking me up for church at 10:30 p.m."

"I am so excited I had to call you. Maureen, I am so happy for you. I hardly slept last night when I think of what Tony did for you. Maureen, that man loves you. You have to come over so we can talk. Maybe a day during the week. You're on vacation this week, aren't you?"

"Yes, I am off this week. I will come over tomorrow. What time will you be in from work?"

"I should be home by 4:00 p.m."

"OK, I will come then. Thanks, Mom. Tony told me he called you and you helped with the planning."

"Yes, it's a good thing you told me he was taking you out for your birthday. Don't forget, I had never met him, but how I see him, girl, he is fine, not to mention caring and a God-fearing man too. I am praying for you guys, but I know you all will make it. I can't believe it, my baby girl getting married. Anyway, go get ready for church, and we will talk tomorrow."

"OK, Mum, thanks for everything. I'll see you tomorrow." I hung up the phone.

I did realize how tired I was; the events of last night really put me in a whirl. I looked at the ring on my finger, so beautiful. So, it wasn't a dream; it really happened, and now I am engaged to be married. It seemed so unbelievable.

Tony is serious about what he says. He went over the top to make my birthday extra special, and then to pop the question at my birthday celebration, that spoke volumes as to how this man is thinking and planning for us.

I got up and made a light breakfast, as maybe from all the excitement, I wasn't feeling very hungry. I was almost dressed by the time Tony called to say he was on his way. He picked me up, and off we went to church.

During the service, Pastor Bradley told the congregation and congratulated his son on his recent engagement to Ms. Maureen Coleman. I could hear a gasp escape the gathering followed by applause and a few "Praise the Lord." He called us up to the front and proceeded to pray for us and blessed us before we returned to our seats.

After service, many people came over to congratulate us. My biggest hug came from Ezra; I don't think he was fully aware of what all this means, but he was happy to see me and, of course, I was coming to his home, and that meant to him playtime.

Unexpectedly, Marion invited us over to lunch, so Tony, Ezra, Aunt Mae, and I all sat down to lunch with Marion and Pastor. Just before lunch, Ezra presented me with his birthday card that he had made. It was a piece of card stock paper folded in half, and he wrote on the front in blue marker, "Happy birthday Miss Maureen." He pasted a bouquet of flower under the writing. On the inside of the card, he pasted a birthday cake on one side and a picture of him on the other side, and he signed it, "Love from your son Ezra."

I gave him a hug and a kiss and thanked him for my card. I told him I love it, and it was the best card anyone ever made for me, and he smiled a bigger smile. We had a lovely afternoon. I enjoyed my meal, and it gave Marion and Pastor an opportunity to tell us all about their trip. We looked at pictures, and Marion gave me a souvenir from the trip.

Before I knew it, it was four thirty, and we got ready to go. Aunt Mae took Ezra home after I promised him, I will come next weekend to play. Tony drove me home and came inside. He hugged and kissed me and told me how beautiful I looked.

"So, what are your plans for your week off?" he asked me.

"I didn't have anything particular in mind. I am going to visit with Mum tomorrow evening and pretty much just catch on chores and little things left undone. Today has been a lovely day, church and lunch with your parents. You are just full of surprises, aren't you?" I said to him with a teasing look.

"Trust me, I had nothing to do with it. Mom must have thought of it at the last minute. Seriously, I have not seen my mom so happy in a long time. From the time I told her I was going to ask you to marry me, she has been smiling and singing and all excited. She and my dad too have taken a real liking to you. Mom knew that I loved you and would have married you once I had gotten myself set up. You know, Maureen, I am very excited about all this too. I don't know if you could understand how I feel, but let me tell you this.

When Robin did her underhanded thing, and Dad made me marry her, we went to city hall. She said she wasn't coming to Brooklyn, and she did not want my father to perform the ceremony. That was fine with me, because at that point, I was angry with him. He made me feel like I was a piece of crap for something that I had no part in creating. For him, there was no middle ground he couldn't take the time to stand by me. Anyway, I went through the ceremony, and I never looked at her, never kissed her, and when I put the ring on her finger, I felt so nauseous as if I would have puked up the place. I'm sorry to sound so harsh, but that was how I felt.

At that time, I hated her. I am not proud of how I felt, but I was angry, hurt, and confused. I couldn't for the life of me understand how I got in the position I was in. It was only after I witnessed the birth of my son that my attitude softened toward her. Living with her through the ordeal of the cancer, birth compassion, and empathy in me toward her, I did the best I could to comfort her and try to make her happy. Within me, you came like a wish that I never thought would come true. (1) You might have never spoke to me again, far less even get back together with me, and (2) you could have been married with a family of your own. In any event, I had resigned myself to the fact that you will never be mine. Now this is like a dream coming true, but I must admit that I wouldn't rest easy until the day we walk down that aisle."

I sat there listening to him; obviously, he felt like he needed to talk. I am sure there is so much he is carrying around within, but then again, I could say the same thing about me.

"Believe it or not, this is like a fantasy for me also," I said to him. "I too figured, at some point, we may have gotten married, but at that time, I was trying to finish my schooling.

Tony, for a couple of years after you left, I wouldn't date anyone because I felt so betrayed by you. Eventually, I did meet someone, and I thought that we would have gotten married, but that didn't work out. When I ran into you, I was trying to deal with the breakup and was deathly afraid to take a chance, especially with you after what happened. It took a whole lot of praying and soul-searching to decide to take a chance. So, I guess both of us have our apprehensions."

"The one thing that I know," Tony said, taking my hand and looking in my face, "if we can put the past behind us, and trust and believe that God is on our side, because I believe that he has brought us together, then we will be fine."

"I agree. I believe that our getting back together is nothing short of a miracle. The way we met at the job and then the park and just the way things have unfolded, it's amazing."

"Anyway, sweetheart," he said, "thank you for a lovely day. Every time we are together, it gets harder to leave you. I want to hold you and love you and have you by my side forever." He kissed my eyes and finally my lips. He got up, raised me up, and wrapped his arms around me. "I love you, baby."

I heard myself say, "I love you too."

"Thank you," he said. "It's music to my ears."

"April," I said, "let's get married the first weekend in April. We got engaged on my birthday, married on your birthday, what do you think?"

"Sounds fantastic. That gives us five months to plan the wedding. Do you want a big wedding, sweetheart?" he asked.

"Not really, close friends and family. I guess your typical traditional wedding."

"Are we going to hire a wedding planner?" Tony asked.

"I don't know yet. I will think about it, and we will decide."

"OK, baby, we will sort it out. Let me run, I have to go see what Ezra's up to and let Aunt Mae go home for a change."

I walked with him to the door, and he kissed me and left.

Five months to get it together before we say "I do." Tomorrow, I will start checking into caterers, limousines, and a venue. I have to decide, do I want bridesmaids and flower girls? As I am thinking over all of this, the phone rang; it was Lisa.

"Good evening, Mrs. Bradley. Where have you been? I tried calling you this morning, and your phone went to voice mail."

"I am sorry, I had the phone off when we were in church. I went to church with Tony this morning."

"That's lovely. You two are acting like an old married couple already, and you are not married yet. Maureen, last night was super. Girl, I couldn't believe it. When he got down on his knee and proposed to you, I started crying. I couldn't stop the tears. The folks at the table may have been wondering why I was crying, but they don't know what I know, and to see it, it stirred up every emotion in me."

"I know that! I couldn't believe it myself. I think I am still asking myself if all of this is possible. Lisa, six months ago, I was going through so much crap with James and how he was acting. At that time, I was so miserable, and now today, six months later, I am engaged. Lisa, do you think we are rushing it?"

"I don't think so. It is obvious that Tony knows what he wants, and that is you. He is not interested in playing games, and believe me, that party had to cost him a pretty penny—that place is not cheap. It tells me the level of caring he has for you. He thinks you are worth it. Maureen, after all you have been through, you deserve the best. You know my mother would say, 'Don't marry the man you love, marry the man that loves you.' And that man loves you."

"He just left not long ago, and we decided that the wedding will be the first Saturday in April," I said.

"OK, let me know what you want me to do. I will be there in whatever capacity you want me to be. Don't worry about a thing. Trust and believe in what God has placed in your way. Put the past behind you and move forward with your life. The road is opening before you. Take hold of the hand of two men on either side of you, Christ on hand and Tony on the next, and walk through your life with them."

"As always, girl, I don't know where you get your advice, but it is always right on. Lisa, I want you to be my maid of honor, so we have to decide on colors. Most likely two Saturdays from now, we'll sit down and talk."

"OK, no problem, but I am telling you right now, don't think of putting me in no pea-green dress or hot pink—I would be so not having it."

"All right, crazy mama, but seriously, do you really think I would choose those colors?"

"I don't know, but just in case, I am telling you right now, I would look so awful in those colors."

"Don't worry, we will come up with a color you like and that I can live with, OK?"

"OK, I will talk with you during the week. Enjoy your week off. Us working people have to go get our clothes ready for tomorrow. I will talk to you later," she said with a snicker.

"Bye, Lisa. Talk to you in a day or so." I hung up the phone. I am going to have my hand full with her and this maid of honor dress, but it will work out. I know how she gets and she knows how I get, so between the two of us, we will come up with a plan that will work for both of us. That's my friend Lisa.

Monday afternoon, as promised, I sat down with Mom. She was so excited and wanted to know how soon we were going to set the date. I told her that we decided on Saturday, April 3, 2010.

"That gives us five months to plan this wedding," she said. "Maureen, I must ask you, do you love him? Are you ready to be a mother to his son?"

"I love him. The more I interact with him, the more all my feelings for him have come back. I love his son as if he was my own. He endeared himself to me from the first day he threw his little arms around my legs. Mom, did I tell you that he named his son after Dad? His name is Ezra."

"Really, how come?"

"Because we had a discussion once, and I said if I have a son, I would name him after my dad. He said he remembered that, and if his plans had worked out, his son would have been our first child, so he named him as we had said."

"Wow, that guy is deep. He must really love you. I am happy for you. All I can tell you is, keep the prayers going. God is turning your life around, and you need to praise him and thank him for his mercy."

"I total agree. For the last four years, I have lived hoping that James would have married me and let us settle down, but it was not to be, and now I understand why."

"Like I told you before, God moves in a mysterious way, his wonders to perform."

"Mom, do you think I should hire a wedding planner?"

"Of course, it's up to you, but I believe that you have people right here that know you and want your day to be special and beautiful. Why don't you ask your friend Diane? I heard you say she knows how to throw a party, and what about Lisa?"

"You know, you could be on to something there. Lisa is crazy, but she has a good heart, and she did say she wanted to help. I think what I will do is have Lisa, Diane, Marion, and you over to my place and let's sit down and lay out everything. After we met, I will decide if we can handle it or if it would be best to hire a planner."

"Sound greats. The holidays are closing on us fast. I would like to invite Tony and Ezra, and Marion and the Pastor to have Thanksgiving with us. Find out from Marion if it's OK to give me her number, and I will call her. I want to call as soon as possible, as I don't know what she may be planning."

"OK. I will speak to her tomorrow. If I had known before, I was over there yesterday. I could have spoken to her then. It's alright. I will call her tomorrow."

The rest of the visit was spent reliving Saturday night and what she wanted to serve for Thanksgiving, with the understanding that I was coming over from the night before to help with the cooking and setup.

Chapter 19

"I have a design for a dress I know will look beautiful on you," Diane said as we sat around my dining table going over plans for the wedding. I had invited Diane, Lisa, Marion, and Mom to sit down and see what had to be done to make this wedding a beautiful day.

"As a matter of fact, I have several designs. You may want to come by the shop and look them over to see if you like any of them."

"OK, how is next weekend?"

"That will be fine. I will have everything ready for you to see."

For the next two hours, we made a list and decided who was doing what. Marion and Mom are going to be looking into catering halls and the menu. They were also going to check out having the invitations printed. Lisa was going to check on the limousines and flowers, and Diane was going to show me her designs for my dress and work on the bridesmaids' and flower girls' dresses. Lisa was going to be my maid of honor, and two of my other girlfriends, Janice and Pat, were going to be bridesmaids. Marion suggested two of her goddaughters to be the flower girls, and of course, Ezra will be the ring bearer. All in all, it was a very fruitful meeting.

Later that evening, Tony called to inquire how the planning meeting went. I rehearsed all that we planned, and I asked him if he had decided on who would be his best man. He said he had asked his friend Ron and he accepted.

"I know that I haven't said it, but my father will be performing the ceremony."

"I figured so. I am sure he and Marion would be disappointed if we didn't have the ceremony in the church."

"You don't mind, do you?"

"Of course not". I replied as reassuring as I could. I guess that question came because of his experience with Robin.

"The only other things that has to be decided on is how we would want the church decorated."

"I am sure when you get through with it, the place is going to be beautiful," he said. I could hear the smile in his voice.

"Looks like we are on our way. I have to decide on the two groomsmen to escort your bridesmaids. I may ask Viv's husband, Rodney, and Shondell's boyfriend, Evan, to be the groomsmen. I also have to decide what type of tuxedo and color we will wear. After the holidays, I have to get together with them and go to the tuxedo shop so we can decide on our look."

"You know, it looks like it's far away, but when January gets here, it will be right at our doorstep," I said.

I know that to be true. It always looks as if you have all the time in the world, but before you know it, the time is gone; and you are left wondering, where did the time go?

"Speaking of holidays," Tony continued, "our office usually has a very nice Christmas party. I don't remember the date right now, but when I do, I will let you know. I would love very much for you to accompany me."

"Hopefully, yes. I can't think of any conflicts, just let me know when you find out the date."

"OK. Good night. We'll talk tomorrow."

"Good night, baby. Kiss Ezra for me."

"Will do," he said and blew me a kiss.

I hung up the phone, and suddenly, I felt overwhelmed.

Just thinking of all that has to be done, it seemed like there is so much to do. Will we really be able to pull this off? It's something I have dreamed of for a long time, and now it is practically here, and I am apprehensive of all that it entails.

I decided to put it out of my head for now. I know the secret to making this affair a success, would be me not allowing myself to be stressed but to approach it calmly, knowing that I want my day be enjoyable and not seem like a chore.

Next week will be Thanksgiving, and we all will be going to Mom's for dinner. We are starting to come together as one big family; I can imagine what it will be like once the grandchildren come along. *OK, Maureen, let's get married first before we start getting the babies,* I chided myself.

I met with Diane as planned, and we looked over several styles. There were all great, but I decided on one gown there that looked absolutely gorgeous. It was antique white satin. The top was long sleeves made entirely of a beautifully designed lace. It left much of my neck and shoulders bare. The lace covered the top of the dress, which was made in a bustier style. The top had a sheer organza that wrapped around part of the top and across part of the dress and then appeared to be held in place by a large rose made of the same material as the dress. The skirt portion of the dress contained lace appliqués. The hemline was covered with lace that continued all around to the train. It was beautiful. I decided that this was the gown I wanted to wear.

We also looked at bridesmaids' dresses, and for the flower girls. I was undecided on whether to go with the electric blue or the papaya color. I have to talk to Tony to see what color he had in mind for the groomsmen—that way, we could be coordinated. Diane said she will get started on the dress after the holidays but will most likely pick up the fabric in another week or so. The next time I visit with her, I will have to have Lisa and the two bridesmaids and the flower girls so we can decide on the color and style of dress.

The night before Thanksgiving, I went over to Mom's and helped her prepare the meal. The menu planned was turkey with stuffing and a mushroom gravy, short ribs of beef, brown stew red snapper, candied yams; collard green; wild rice; tossed salad; pumpkin pie and apple pie; and homemade biscuits. It was quite a bit, but Mom always wants to make sure that people have choices, and if they want to take a care package home, there will be enough for them to do so.

We never got to bed until 2:00 a.m. We were back up by 7:00 a.m. We told everyone to come at 4:00 p.m., and everything was ready when they arrived. We had an enjoyable evening, talking and laughing. Mom and Marion had more time to talk. Dad met Ezra, and the two of them hit it off right away. At one time, we missed the guys, and they were all watching a game and talking all sports. By nine, the people started to leave, and I stayed and help Mom clean up. I had asked Steven for the day off, as I just knew that I was going to be dog tired at the end of this dinner. Once everything was packed away, I went to bed and was asleep in nothing flat.

Midweek, Mom called to say she and Marion had an appointment to meet with the manager of a catering hall. She said they had identified three places that they thought would be ideal, and they will get all the particulars to share them with Tony and me. They had also contacted a print shop on Utica Avenue and would be going over there to see a selection of invitations, again I asked her to bring samples for us to decide on. As I hung up the phone, I thought to myself, these two moms are getting along just great.

Both of them have such love for their children and would want to see them happy. While a wedding planner may go about things from a professional level, these two women had their emotions involved. They wanted our wedding days to be the best. I know for Marion, the fact that she feels that Tony will finally be marrying the woman that he loves makes her happy.

One of the things that had not been discussed is finances. It should have been the top of the list. As I thought about it, I wondered if I should call Mom back and hear what she had to say. I picked up the phone, and I called.

"Mom," I said, "you know I have not discussed the cost of the wedding with Tony. How should I bring up the subject to him? Do you have any idea of who should pay what?"

"You know, just last night, your father and I were discussing the same thing. We feel that we should do our part. We decided that we will give you your wedding dress—well, I should say your whole ensemble, dress, veil, shoes."

"That sounds beautiful. Did I tell you that I decided on one of the designs that Diane showed me? It's beautiful, Mom! Diane said she will begin making it in January."

"I can't wait to see it, but I will wait on until you have a fitting to take a look at it. I think the catering hall and the price of the plates will be your biggest expense. Do you have any idea how much guests you are going to have?"

"I am figuring at least a hundred. I see where I am going to have to sit with Tony and discuss this. I don't know how many friends he might want to invite, but I really don't see us going over a hundred."

"The sooner the better, and you two have to start getting a list together and decide on a figure for the guest list."

"Mom, this is a lot to do, isn't it? I wanted to get married for a while now, but now that it's here, I am realizing that this is work, especially if you want your day to be special."

"My dear, you don't have to worry," Mom said. "It is all going to work out, and you are going to have the dream wedding you deserve. Once you give us the information we need and our suggestions meet your approval, you don't have to worry about anything else, it will be taken care of. Embrace your life, look forward to your day with happiness in your heart, not dread or uncertainty. That day, you are going to be a beautiful bride, and that beauty will shine if within you are happy and have the confidence that the people who love you have been there for you and have done everything in their power to make your day complete."

"You are making this thing sound so easy, but I know that you will be there for me."

"Another thing," Mom continued, "don't be afraid to talk to your husband-to-be. Start from how to be open about things that are or will affect you both. Don't wait on him to do everything or suggest everything. If something has to be addressed, you bring it to him. Your husband is not a mind reader, and neither are you, so don't expect him to know what you are thinking or needing. It's all in how you do things. Respect each other, and trust me, you will have a good marriage."

"Thanks, Mom. I appreciate all that you are saying to me. I will talk with Tony."

"OK, my darling, I am not trying to overwhelm you, but sometimes, as things are laid on my heart, I give it to the person it's intended for. We'll talk later. Love you. Bye."

She hung up the phone. I guess it's so much to being a wife and mother. I feel blessed and happy because I know that I have the support of my family, and I even feel to some extent that I will have the support of Tony's family as well. Mom is right; I need to embrace life and look forward to my day with joy. Yes, there will be little glitches, adjustments may have to be made here and there, but in the end, I want to enjoy my day, for I have been waiting a long time for it to come.

Chapter 20

One week before Christmas arrives. Admittedly, I wasn't thinking about doing too much for the holidays. The wedding had taken center stage. Each passing week moved it closer and closer. This evening, I was going over to Tony's to help decorate the Christmas tree.

Earlier in the day, we had selected a live tree from a vendor on Linden Boulevard. I also wanted to pick up some decorations, so I told him I will get them from a big discount store on Pennsylvania Avenue, which had the biggest selection of Christmas ornaments.

Yearly, the store had beautifully decorated trees on display. The trees were decorated in the traditional red and green, but others were done in blue, silver, or ribbons. I particularly wanted to decorate our tree like the silver and ribbon one they had on display. I thought it was really gorgeous. I picked up the silver flowers, silver ornaments and the ribbon I would need to create a replica of the tree.

I planned to arrive at six so we could have dinner together, and then we would decorate the tree. I wondered if I should bring Ezra's present and put it under the tree, but knowing how kids react to presents, I thought it best to leave it until Christmas Eve that way, he would not be tempted to open it to sneak a peek.

I called Tony as I parked in front of the house, and by the time I got out the car, he appeared at the door. He came down the steps to help me with the bags, and we hurried in out of the cold.

Once inside the house, Ezra greeted me, all excited,

"Miss Maureen, Dad bought a big Christmas tree. Come, let me show you."

He took my hand and led me to the living room. Tony had already set it up; all that was needed was to put the lights and the decoration.

"Wow, it's beautiful," I said, wanting to share in the excitement with him. Of course, he didn't know that I was there when the tree was bought.

"OK, Ezra," his dad said, "let us have our dinner first, and afterward, we will decorate the tree."

"Yeah, OK, let's eat," he said and headed to the dining room.

Tony had placed all the bags in the living room and indicated to me to follow him. We went into the kitchen, and it was filled with the scent of something cooking.

"Who's cooking?" I said, knowing full well that he said he was going to be making dinner.

"Oh, you're funny," he said with a smirk. "Prepare to have your taste buds tantalized."

He had made curry okra with salted codfish, white sweet potatoes, and sweet plantains. We brought the food to the table, we sat down, he said grace, and we ate.

"I have never had okra and codfish like this—it's good. Who taught you how to cook?"

"Mom, of course. You know my grandmother was from Jamaica, so I enjoyed many a sweet potatoes, yam, and plantains from her when I was growing up.

You remember I was skinny in college? Well, Grandma used to tell my mom, 'You have to give that boy some plantain or cornmeal porridge and strengthen him up.' Whenever we stayed at her house, you know that's what she would feed me."

We both laughed.

"So, are you making cornmeal or plantain porridge for Ezra?"

"I have made the various porridges and tried to get him to drink them but he doesn't care for it. I usually end up drinking it. He does like oatmeal and farina, so I don't stress him with the other stuff."

With the meal finished, we cleaned up the kitchen and started on the tree. He put on a Christmas CD, and we worked on the tree. We sang along with the songs and had fun. We had bought a seven-foot tree, as the house has high ceiling, and we had to get the step ladder so Tony could hoist Ezra up to put the star on. That was the finishing touch, and then we turned on the lights. It was beautiful.

We turned off the overhead light and let the tree lights light up the room. As Tony cleared away the boxes and bags, I sat on the sofa, and Ezra came and sat by me. I reached over and pulled him into my arms, putting him to rest his head in my lap while we looked at the blinking lights.

Once Tony was finished cleaning up, he came and sat next to me, slipping his hand around my neck kissing me on my ear, and whispered, "I love you."

I turned and kissed his lips and said, "I love you too." We sat there, listening to music and watching the lights. Ezra would talk, but before long, I didn't hear a word out of him, and I realize he had fallen asleep.

Tony lifted him from my lap and took him up to his room. I went along to help turn down his bed while Tony undressed him and put his pj's on him. Once tucked into bed, I kissed him good night, as did Tony.

"Maureen, do you want something to drink?" Tony asked as we returned to the living room.

"You could make me my favorite," I said, resuming my seat on the sofa. Tony came in and handed me the drink, sitting down beside me.

"You did a beautiful job on the tree, soon-to-be Mrs. Bradley. Going forward, you are the official tree decorator of the Bradley family Christmas tree."

"Thank you, Mr. Bradley, for bestowing such a prestigious title on me." He reached over and pulled me into his arms.

"The best title I can give you will be Mrs. Maureen Bradley, four months and counting."

"Tony, I know we haven't talked about the finance associated with the wedding, but my parents are giving me my wedding clothes, gown, veil, etc. Of course, we don't know how much the catering will cost, and I figure that will be our highest expense. I think we may have to keep the guest list to a hundred. What do you think?"

"I think 100, maybe 120, will be sufficient. I know my mom will want to invite a couple of her close friends. When will the invitations be going out?"

"The moms are working on them. I would think that they should be out by at least the first week in February."

"By then, we will have the list together, and we will make sure it doesn't exceed that number. I will be taking care of the catering. My parents have also said that they will give $5,000 to help with flowers and the limousines. If there is any shortfall, I will take care of it."

"What do I have to contribute?"

"I don't believe you need to contribute anything, except being here, and when the preacher asks if you will accept this man as your lawfully wedded husband, say 'I will.'"

"You are funny," I said with a laugh. "I think I should help out in some way financially."

"Well, don't forget, you have to have your hair done, manicure, pedicure. I'm sure you are going to want pick up things for the honeymoon. Speaking of which, we haven't even talked about that yet. All of that could be your expense."

"OK, this is a lot to do, isn't it?"

"Yeah, but when you consider that we are only doing this one time, we could as well have a day to remember for the rest of our lives. I can't wait for that day to get there, to finally have you all to myself. When he asks me if I will love her, cherish her, and keep her only so long as I may live, I am going to answer loudly, 'I will.'"

As we talked, my head was resting on his chest. I could feel his heart beating, and I wondered how much love was in that heart for me? Does this man love me so deeply as evidenced by the things he has done, planned to do, and says? I could feel this overwhelming feeling of love stirred within me, and I stood up and stretched out my hands, taking his and pulling him up from the sofa. I put my arms around his back and just moved to the rhythm of the music that was playing.

His arms encircled my waist, he lowered his head and started to kiss me, my hair, my ears, and all along my neck. His lips finally found mine; his tongue in my mouth was so sweet. I could feel my body start to tremble slightly, his hands caressing my back.

"Maureen, I want you so badly, but I will stop if you want me to."

"I don't want you to," I whispered.

"Oh god, baby, you're sure?"

"Yes, I am sure," my hand reaching up to start unbuttoning his shirt. Without another word, he took my hand and led me up the stairs to his bedroom.

Once inside, he closed the door and locked it. He continued to kissed me and then pulled my sweater over my head. His hands moved to unbuttoned my jeans and he pulled them down my legs. Putting me to sit on the bed, he pulled them off completely, leaving me in my bra and panties.

I stood up to help him unbutton his shirt; he finished it off and just as quickly removed his pants. He lifted me up and placed me in the middle of the bed, his eyes glued to my face.

"God, girl, you're so beautiful." He rained kisses all along my chest, onto my breast, his hand caressing my stomach and my legs, his lips kissing me all along my waist line.

With both hands, he pulled the panties off and just looked at me. Taking his hand, he gently brushed all along my hair line and down to my legs. I could see his briefs bulging with his manhood wanting to be free. I reached over to pull at the briefs, but he took care of it for me, pulling it off to set himself free and to enter me. A gasp escaped my lips, and I heard the sharp intake of his breath as he buried the full length of himself into me. The sound that escaped his lip was the sound of pent-up emotions and passion finally being released. He slowed himself down and, reaching his hand behind my back, unhooked my bra. His lips covered my breast, my neck and my face. He took his time, looking for and waiting for the cue from me that will tell him where I was.

The intensity of his lovemaking, the kissing, the holding, the sheer beauty of the moment took hold of me, and I heard myself saying, "Tony, baby, oh god, baby," and I knew I was there. He knew I was here also. I know he was holding on to make sure I was satisfied, and now that he knew, he let all his emotions take hold of him. His cry of surrender went on for a minute. It was as if every emotion, all his passion that had been buried deep in his being, all the want and desire that had been suppressed for years overtook him, wrapped and twisted him in its wake. I knew that he had experienced something that he wanted and hoped for a long time. I wrapped my arms around his back, and I held him as tightly as I could. It was my way of saying, *"I understand, and it's all right."*

"I love you, Tony," I said to him softly.

"I love you too, always did and always will." He rolled onto his side and lay there for a minute before pulling me into his arms and kissing my cheek.

"Thank you, babe" he said. You have no idea how I feel right now. I may never let you out of this bed ever. It's as if I have been in a desert, dried and parched for a long time, and you are like the rain that has fallen on me to give life back to my soul. Sweetheart, I hope you are satisfied. I couldn't hold on any longer. There was too much emotions going through me."

"I am satisfied. I understand what you are saying. There was a lot going through me too."

I lay wrapped in his arms, all the old hurt and doubts no longer in my mind. I could feel his body relax, and from the way he breathes, I could tell that he had fallen asleep. I looked in his face, and I thought about how much he had been through from the last time we made love to this present time.

Looking at him, his eyes closed, his face beautiful and so vulnerable, I wanted to hold him close forever. I closed my eyes and just let the moment surround me. I could hear the rain falling outside, and I wondered when it started. My mind drifted over the past years and all that I have been through myself and all the things that have happened in the past months and found myself saying a prayer, thanking God for his mercies.

I know what Tony said about us waiting until we got married, to be intimate and maybe we should have, but I don't think it mattered. This right here, right now, is real, and I don't feel ashamed. I am happy, and it just cemented my feelings for him even more.

Tony stirred and kissed my face.

"Sorry, babe, I drifted off. It's all that sweetness you laid on me."

"Oh really, if you say so," I said with a smile. We were face-to-face, lying and looking at each other.

"What time is it?" I asked.

He turned and looked at the cable box. "It's 11:30p.m."

"It's time for me to leave," I said.

"Maureen, please stay. It's raining outside, and I really don't want you driving and then having to find a parking in the rain. I think you should stay."

"Do you think it's a good idea? What about Ezra? What if Aunt Mae comes and sees me here? I know we are engaged, but should we do it?"

"Aunt Mae is not a problem. On weekends, she usually calls to see if she needs to come over. I will tell her not to come. Ezra, he probably wouldn't connect the dots, but I'll tell you what—he is usually up by seven, seven thirty. If you want, you can go into the guest bedroom— that way, when he comes into my room in the morning as he usually does, he will not see you there. Bear in mind that I am saying all of this based on your concerns. But as far as I am concerned, you have all rights to be here and don't feel any kind of way about it. We haven't gotten that official piece of paper that says we are man and wife, but you are my wife, and should have been my wife a long time ago, so I am not worried about anything, but I understand your concerns about how you may be perceived."

"Thank you, babe. I will stay and do the guest-room thing," I replied, looking all prim and proper. We both laughed out.

"Sssh," I said, "before you wake up Ezra."

He got out of the bed. "We have to go downstairs and turn off the tree lights. Let's have a cup of tea. I have worked up an appetite for something to eat, but most of all, a big one for you."

He opened the closet and handed me one of his robes. He also put on his, and together we went downstairs. We sat at the kitchen table and had tea with crackers and cheese. Once finished, we turned off the lights and went back to bed and to a night filled with love by two people who had lost it but found it again.

Chapter 21

"Happy New Year, darling," I said to Tony as all around us, everyone was clasping and cheering.

"Happy New Year to you too," he replied, giving me a kiss to the lips and a tight hug.

It was midnight. The ball had dropped in Times Square, and people were celebrating the beginning of a new year. We had attended New Year's Eve service at the church, and afterward, everyone had gone downstairs to a celebration. My mom and dad had come for the first time to the church and joined us to help celebrate.

The year 2010 was here. Maybe it's me, but the time seems to be moving rapidly. It was just a week ago that it was Christmas, and now it's New Year's Eve.

We celebrated Christmas with Tony's family, and we had a wonderful day. That evening, I went over to Tony's, and we opened our gifts.

The highlight of the event was the joy on Ezra's face as he eagerly tore the wrapping off to get to the present. His cries of delight at receiving toys that he wanted or did not expect to get filled the air.

The innocence of children as they experience pure joy is so uplifting to behold. I often wonder when do we lost that innocence. Somewhere in our lives, we grow up, and as we grow, we either lose or forget it.

Being together for Christmas, we already felt like a family; it's moments like this that I have thought of and hoped for a long time. Ezra's happiness gave us joy. To see his little face all aglow made it all worthwhile. I could say that he is one lucky and blessed little boy.

"He cleaned up like a bandit." I thought to myself. He had at least ten gifts to unwrap. He received presents from his dad, his grandparents, my parents, Aunt Mae, his aunts, his godparents, and me. He was happy, happy.

I bought Tony a gold chain with a cross pendant. The design on the cross was unique, and I had his first name engraved on the back. He bought me a pair of topaz and gold earrings.

That night, after we finally put Ezra to bed, we sat in the living room among all the toys and wrapping. After the full day that we had, we decided that we could clean up the living room tomorrow. As Christmas fell on a Friday, we were both off for the weekend, so we decided to spend it together.

Tony left the room for a minute, and when he returned, he handed me a jewelry box.

"What's this?" I said, "You got me another gift?"

"This was my grandmother's who left it for me when she died. I would like for you to wear it on our wedding day."

I took the box, not really knowing what to say and not knowing what to expect. I opened the lid; my mouth flew open.

"Oh my gosh, Tony, this is beautiful. Wow!"

It was an emerald and diamond necklace with matching earrings.

"This was my grandmother's prized possession," he said. Her husband, my grandfather, was a merchant seaman, and he told her he bought it in India on one of his trips. He used to spend months away on those trips. Eventually, he retired, and you know what was so sad? —he died within a year of retiring. He made the money so that they could have a lovely home and be comfortable, but he never got to enjoy it."

"It is stunning. I don't know what to say. Thank you seems inadequate."

"My grandmother loved me, not to say she didn't love the others, but maybe because I was her first grandchild. She died the first year I was in college. My mom said she told her that this was to be given me so I could give it to my wife, the same way her husband gave it to her. My mother has kept it all this time for me, and now I am giving it to my wife so she can wear it on our wedding day."

"Tony, this is so incredible. I will wear it. Thank you."

"Here, turn around," he said; with that, he took it out of the box and fastened it around my neck. I walked to the nearest mirror, and I looked at myself, the gold and green against my skin, so lovely. I removed my earrings from my ears and replaced them with the earrings from the set. Tony came up behind me.

"You look radiant. I can just imagine how you are going to look on that day. I am praying that God will keep us safe and throw his arms of protection around us that everything will go as planned and there will be no obstacles in our way."

He put his arms around my waist, his head resting on my shoulder, as we gazed into the mirror. Silently, as he prayed, I was praying right along with him, praying that the love that we feel so strongly for each other will never diminish or leave us—that all will go smoothly and that we approach the day with love and a commitment to care for each other.

Now it was New Year's, and that meant the holidays were over; now the work begins. We have three months to put it all together.

I went over and greeted my mom and dad, wishing them a Happy New Year. Next was Marion and Pastor, everyone with smiles on their faces and wishing all the best for the New Year.

When I got close to my mom, I told her that we have to sit down and start getting the guest list together. I told her that Tony and I will make a decision on the style of the invitations based on the samples that they brought us.

She agreed and said that we should get together an evening in the week if I wanted to, or it could wait till weekend.

The rest of the night was spent eating, dancing, and just enjoying the company. Tony dropped me home, and we said that we would see each other later in the day.

That weekend, Mom, Marion, Tony, and I sat down at Marion's house and went over the wording for the invitations. We decided on the style and the wording. The invitation will read as follows:

Mr. & Mrs. Ezra Coleman
and
Rev. Dr. & Mrs. Joseph Bradley
invite you to share in the joy of the marriage of their children
Maureen Yvette Coleman
&
Anthony David Bradley
on Saturday, April 2, 2010,
at
4 o'clock in the afternoon
Tabernacle of Praise
The Church of Living God
570 Thomas Boyland Street
Brooklyn, New York 11212

Just reading it sent shivers up my spine. We chose the soft beige paper with a design of interlocking hearts on the front. We also decided on the venue, which was the beautiful Venetian Rose Hall located in Park Slope. I had been there to a wedding about two years ago, and the ambience, the service, and the food were excellent. It was a bit pricey, but they were willing to work with us.

We had a meeting schedule with them two weeks from now to finalize figures and menu choices. The next thing, of course, was getting the guest list together, and we started. We each created a list, which included family, friends, and associates. Once we counted the names, we were at 115. We wanted to stay at that number, but definitely no more than 120. By the time we ended, we had accomplished all that we set out to do. Marion suggested that there is a sister from the church who was very good at decorating and that she could be willing to decorate the church. All we have to do is let her know if we wanted any specific design; if not, we could leave it up to her and give her the supplies she would need to do the job. I told Marion I would be willing to meet with her to discuss it.

The next thing to take care of would be my dress, the bridesmaids', Maid of Honor's, and the flower girls'. I had spoken to Diane during the week, and she said that she had started on it and should be able to have the first fitting a week from then.

Tony and I spoke briefly on the honeymoon, which also has to be planned. We have to make a decision, as tickets will have to be booked with the airlines and hotel stay arranged. So far, we had talked about going to one of the Caribbean islands, either St. Lucia or Jamaica. We were also considering Miami Beach as a possibility.

As I am getting deeper into this, I could see how it could become overwhelming. I was determined to take it all in stride.

I remember when my girlfriend Heather got married. She was running around for months, and she had a wedding planner. I would never forget when I spoke to her about a week before the wedding, and she told me that she was so tired of everything that she could not wait to get the day over with. I remember thinking to myself that it was one of the saddest things I had heard. I couldn't imagine that a person's wedding day could become such a chore and a burden that they just wanted to get it over with. I wondered if she enjoyed her wedding, or was she so worn out at that point that the joy had left the occasion?

I was determined not to let that happen to me. I plan to enjoy my day. I know that I am fortunate and blessed for the people that are supporting me. They are prepared to help me through this, and they want it be a joyous time for me. I am going to accept their help and be thankful for it.

We finally settled on honeymooning in Miami Beach. The travel agent had shown us several lovely hotels on Collins Avenue, and we decided on the Marriott in South Beach. The area offered a lot of nightlife and attractions that we could do. We will leave the Sunday after the wedding and return that Friday. Doing it that way, we will have the weekend to recuperate, because we would both be back to work by the Monday.

Another thing that I will have to deal with is my apartment. My lease runs until June. I planned to talk with my landlady to see if there will be a problem with me breaking the lease. Chances are I will keep the apartment until the end of May, which would give me time to dispose of stuff and move things over to Tony's.

As these things unfold before me, I am realizing that this is such a serious step that I am taking. I have lived with someone before, for the months James and I were together, but I had not lived with Tony, and in addition to that, I will have a child to take care of.

I think that my feelings of anxiety are natural. Marriage is a big step, it will be no longer about me, but it will be about us. After the wedding, then comes the day-to-day living, and that is the part that is most scary for me.

In spite of all my little apprehensions, I feel confident that it will all work out. I know that I have people around me that care enough, will give me good advice, and I can talk to anytime if I feel a little overwhelmed. Right now, I am trying not to overthink and think too far ahead. With a little over two months to go, I have set up a timetable of events so as to be able to stay on top of what has to be done—that way, in all the excitement, I don't forget.

Chapter 22

"Maureen, the limousine will be here in the next twenty minutes," Mom said.

"I'll be ready. I have only to put on my gown. Everything else is done."

"The photographer is downstairs waiting to start taking the pictures also. We have to make time for him before the car gets here," Mom continued.

I started to answer her when my phone rang.

"Hello, darling. How are you doing?" It was Tony.

"Isn't it bad luck to see the bride before the wedding?" I said with a big smile on my face.

"Could be, I don't know. I can't see you, but I am talking to you. I am trying to pinch myself to see if this day is really here. Are you nervous? I am! Are you dressed yet?"

"Almost, just have to put on my gown, and we will take some photos. The limo will be there in about fifteen minutes, so I have to get moving."

"Yes, my darling, I will see you shortly. I love you, babe. Bye." He hung up. Mom appeared in the doorway just as I hung up the phone.

I decided to get dressed at my parents' house. I think it's traditional for the bride to leave her parents' home. I spent the night before here. I slept in my old room, and Mom and I got up early in the morning and had breakfast together. We checked over everything that was scheduled for today, and we entrusted it to God's hands. As far as we were concerned, everything was ready. All we had to do is be at the church at the appointed time. I had an appointment at ten to have my hair done, and I also had a facial, but I wanted to do my own makeup.

"OK, let me help you into your gown, time is gone. I know it's fashionable for the bride to be late, but let's not have people waiting for hours. Not to mention, your groom will probably have a fit, thinking you stood him up at the altar."

She helped me, and the gown was on; it fitted perfectly. She fastened the necklace Tony asked me to wear around my neck, and I put on the earrings. At that point, Mom called the photographer upstairs, and he began taking shots as she helped me to put my veil on. We did several poses, and then Dad came and joined us for a couple more shots.

As we were wrapping it up, my brother called out that the limousine was outside. I had ordered the white Excalibur, the one that plays "Here Comes the Bride." One final look in the mirror, and I was satisfied that everything was in order. I walked outside to the waiting limo. Dad, Mom, and my brother's girlfriend all were helping to make sure that the dress and the train were protected. I got in the car, and Dad closed the door. They would be following me in the other limo.

I sat back, and my journey began. Just now, as Dad closed the door, I thought, *He has just closed the door on my old life, and when the door reopens, I will begin my new life.*

As I traveled, my mind went back to the last three months. It started out slow, but it soon sped up—all the preparation, the decisions, the fittings, the rehearsals, and the anxiety.

About three weeks ago, my bridesmaid Pat said she could no longer do it. I was sorry she had to drop out, and it meant having to find someone at this late date. Charlie's girlfriend, Monica, said she would do it, and Diane had to get busy, altering the dress to fit. Thank God that worked out. The color I chose for the bridesmaids and flower girls was cerulean blue. The groomsmen are wearing cream suits with the vest, tie, and lapel kerchief of that color. Lisa's dress is the same color but designed differently. They are off-the-shoulder gowns. The top portion of the dress looked pleated, and a rosette of the same fabric sits just above the left breast. The design was truly lovely. The flower girls' dresses were adorable. Their dresses were made with a cap sleeve, and flowers of the same color were placed in their hair.

When Mom came to see me in the final fitting, she broke down and starting crying. She made me cry also; it is just that she was so happy for me. She had watched my life for the last four years I was with James, and while she did not know all that I went through with him, to see how happy I am with Tony and how Tony has treated me and now to make me his wife, she couldn't hold it in any longer. I told her to do all her crying now, because on my day, I wanted no tears, only smiles and happiness.

Lisa threw me a bridal shower. I felt like I didn't have the time for it, but I realized that she cares for me and just wanted me to enjoy this occasion, so I got caught up in all the hype, and it turned out to be fantastic. Lisa dug up so many of our old college friends; I have no idea how she did it. She had a lingerie show as part of the shower. The idea being that I could chose lingerie for my wedding night and my honeymoon. I got in the spirit of things and modeled a couple of pieces that I liked. I enjoyed my evening.

Tony had a bachelor's party of sort. He had the fellers over to his man's cave, the basement, and he said it was great.

We traveled from East New York to the church. I was twenty minutes late; there was a bit of traffic along the way, but eventually, I pulled up in front the church. I waited for Mom and Dad to pull up also, and they came to help me out the car. As I got in the church, the whole bridal party was there, and we began to line up. Marion came up to me, she gave me a slight hug.

"I don't want to crush anything. You look so beautiful, my dear. I know you all are going to be very happy. She handed me a small white lacy handkerchief. This was my handkerchief I had from my wedding; it came in handy once the tears of joy filled my eyes. You may need it."

"Thank you, Marion." I reached out and took it from her and squeezed her hand. "Thank you very much. I am hoping I don't cry."

Lisa walked up to me, the biggest smile on her face.

"Maureen, girl, I am about to cry this place down. You look gorgeous. It's here, Maureen, it's finally here." I took her hand.

"Listen, Lisa, I need you to be strong for me. You know it doesn't take much to make me cry, but I don't want to look a mess, mascara running, eyes red. You know we both look awful when we cry, so don't even think about it."

"I'll do my best, but it's not going to be easy."

I heard Diane's voice calling everyone to attention so we could line up for the procession to begin. We had rehearsed this enough, so everyone knew where they were supposed to be.

Everyone finally lined up, and the procession began. As I entered and started walking down the aisle on the arm of my father, I could see all the smiling faces, and the church looked so beautiful, and at the end of the aisle stood the man who turned to watch me as I approached.

The choir and congregation sang "Lead Us Heavenly Lead Us." It really wasn't that long a walk, but I felt like I was walking a mile. His eyes fixed on me; every step I took brought me closer to him, and eventually, I stood next to him. Lisa reached over and took my bouquet. My dad lifted my veil, and I turned to face Tony.

The smiles on both our faces, I was so happy, and it all felt unreal. He took my hand and we faced Pastor Bradley. For the next twenty minutes, the ceremony unfolding, we repeated our vows and exchanged rings. The last thing Pastor Bradley said was "By the power vested in me by the state of New York, I now pronounce you man and wife. You may kiss your bride."

He took me in his arms, and he whispered to me, "I will love you forever," and then he kissed me. We turned to face our guests, who clapped and cheered.

We walked down the aisle. As I walked, happiness filled my being, all the months of planning, all the anxiety, all the apprehension, all gone. I am now Mrs. Maureen Bradley. Father God, thank you.

From the church, the bridal party went to Grand Army Plaza to the Water Fountain to take pictures. We were lucky the weather outside was mild, considering that it was early April. We took a series of shots and then went on to the reception. At one point, after all the speeches and toasts and finally dinner, Ezra came up to me.

"Miss Maureen, are you my mommy now? Daddy said that today you were going to become my mommy."

I looked at him, and I reached over and hugged him.

"Yes, I am your mommy now. So, from now on, no more Miss Maureen—it's Mommy." He threw his arms around me, and I looked up and realized Tony was watching us, and he came and made it a group hug.

"You are going to make a supermom, and I cannot wait to have you all to myself, I am so ready to take you away so we can be alone," he said as he led me to the dance floor.

We joined other couples on the floor dancing, his arms around my waist and his head resting on my head, and we just moved to the music. I could feel him kissing me along the side of my face, my ears, his body moving, so inviting against mine. He is right; I cannot wait until we are all alone.

Soon it was time to remove the garter. Tony had me blushing. There I was sitting in the middle of the floor, and he took my gown and covered his head. I could hear the guests gasp then laughter. It was only a minute, but he was funny. I covered my face, smiling and blushing from ear to ear. He retrieved the garter, and then he tossed it to all guys who were willing to try to catch it.

I didn't know the guy who caught it, but it looked like his girlfriend was excited. I heard her squealing and clapping. I guess, to her, that meant she was getting married soon. I hope she would be as lucky as I felt right now. Then came the bouquet toss, and a friend of mine Sylvia caught it. She was excited, and she jumped up and a down a couple of times before running over to her boyfriend. I am hoping for the best for her also. We cut the cake and fed each other and kissed. Everything was just fantastic. I had no idea when I was going to get off of cloud nine.

I had Mom holding on to all the envelopes we received. We walked from table to table to greet our guests and take a picture with the table. Everything just flowed into place.

Eventually, the last dance was danced, and the reception ended. Tony, Ezra, Aunt Mae, and I got into the limousine to take us to Tony's house. We chatted as we drove along, and Ezra sat next to me. He rested his head in my lap, and before we got home, he was asleep.

Once we arrived home, Tony lifted him out of the car and took him inside. Aunt Mae wished me good night and hugged me and told me to tell Tony she went home to her bed. By the time I got up the steps, Tony came out to meet me.

"You didn't think I was going to let you walk in to your new home without me there to welcome you in?" He stood in the doorway, extended his hand, and assisted me to step inside.

"Welcome home, Mrs. Bradley."

Once inside, his arm went around my waist, and he just hugged me tightly. "Finally, my wife," he said. "Praise God." I realized he had laid Ezra on the sofa, and now that we were in, he proceeded to take Ezra upstairs to bed.

I followed him up the stairs and helped him put on Ezra's pajama and put him under the covers. We both kissed him good night, and we walked into our bedroom. When he opened the door, the room was beautiful. There were vases of flowers placed throughout the room. The bed was covered with flower petals. Someone has decorated the room.

"Tony, did you do all this?"

"Yes, I want my bride to know how much I love her, and nothing is too good for her."

"You are incredible. What am I going to do with you?"

"Just love me," he replied, "as I love you."

"Deal, all my love and more just for you." I slipped my hand around his neck, looking into his face.

"Sit on the bed," he said. I sat. He knelt on the floor and, taking my ankle, removed my shoe. "Nice, but that's the way it should be for these lovely feet." He removed the other shoe. He got up and raised me up, turned me around, and unzipped the dress. I let it fall to the floor, and he helped me step out of it.

"My turn," I said. I motioned for him to sit on the bed, and I too removed his shoes. I then moved to the jacket and the vest; he helped with the tie, and I continued with the shirt. He unbuckled his belt, and I zipped down his pants, which he also allowed to fall to the floor. All our wedding clothes were now in a heap on the floor.

"Let's take a shower," he said, taking hold of my hand and heading to the bathroom. We removed our undergarments, and once we set the water, we stepped into the shower.

We washed each other's skin between kisses. I washed the makeup off my face, and we brushed our teeth before returning to the bedroom.

The feel of the flower petals on my skin, the kisses of my husband as he started from my feet to my head, just loving me, the way he looked at me as he slowly made love to me. The smell of the flowers and the glow from the flameless candles that were spread out around the room made my wedding night a night I will never forget. Needless to say, I never did get to wear the lingerie that I had picked out for my wedding night. I don't think he would have even noticed it. His whole focus was just on me, not what I was wearing, and he would have wanted it off anyhow.

Chapter 23

"Hello, Mrs. Bradley"; it was Lisa calling. "I have hardly been hearing from you. How is married life?"

"Hectic," I replied, "full-time wife and mother now."

"Happy four-month anniversary. Today is four months since you walked down the aisle."

"Really, it seems like it was just last week. Technically, I am still on my honeymoon, you know."

"Well, excuse us poor unmarried folk. We are not privy to such information." She burst out laughing.

"I know. I am being so mean to my best friend, I am sorry," I said with a smile in my voice. It's all good. "Seriously, Lisa, I have been a bit busy getting used to the routine of caring for a child. I had to deal with my first temper tantrum the other day. I am developing a whole new outlook on parenting."

"I know you will be able to handle it. You have resources. You have your mom, and you have Marion and Aunt Mae—she had been raising him for a while. I am sure she will be of help."

"She most definitely is helping. If I didn't have her to help me out in the mornings, I would be wearing a wig by now."

"Well, you are on your way. Keep up the good work, and just don't forget me."

"Let's meet for lunch a day next week. It's summer. We could walk over to Metro Tech and eat outdoors."

"Sounds great. Call and let me know what day you want to do it."

"Will do. OK, we'll talk later," I said.

"OK. Bye," Lisa said and hung up.

Four months already, I can't believe it. I really do still feel like a newlywed. Every month so far on our anniversary date, Tony has been bringing me flowers.

Sometimes in my quiet time, I have relived our wedding and our honeymoon. We finally got the DVD and the CD of the wedding. From the CD, we will have to decide which pictures we want to make up our wedding album. At some point, we are going to have to sit down and make the selections.

Our honeymoon was fantastic; we went off to Miami Beach the day after. Our days were filled with swimming and making love, and we managed to visit two clubs in the area and danced until they closed. We went over to the shops in Bal Harbor and had fun looking at all the designer clothes.

I finally got to wear the lingerie I had picked out for my wedding night, although it wasn't on for long. Tony loved the pieces I had selected, and it gave him even more joy peeling them off me. We both said that it all felt like a dream because we never knew that we could be so happy.

One of the things I discovered about Tony is that he prays consistently. He makes a quiet time to pray in the morning and at night. He says a prayer before eating, doesn't matter where we are, he holds my hand and bless our meal. This was new to me. I must confess that I didn't pray every day, and sometimes at night, I would go to sleep without praying. Now he made me aware of how important it is to pray.

We discussed my coming off the pill, so I had stopped taking the pill just before we got married. At this point, I know that it will take my body time to adjust, so my GYN doctor told me not to worry; some women get pregnant soon after stopping, while it may take longer for other women.

I am not rushing; whenever it happens, I will be happy. We have been going to church like a family every Sunday, and I am slowly getting accustomed to my new church family.

Yesterday morning, Tony was not feeling well, which is so unlike him. Something upset his stomach, and he was so nauseous, he vomited. He went to work, and he said he felt better as the day wore on. I myself have had a little stomach cramp, and I wondered if my period is on its way. They have been a little irregular since coming off the pill, and so far, I calculated that they are late right now. I planned that after work this evening, I would stop by the pharmacy and pick up a pregnancy test kit. In a way, I am looking forward to having a baby; it has been my dream for a long time.

I am not sure why I have such a love of children. I have seen mothers with their babies, and I had always hoped that one day, I will be blessed with one of my own. I didn't want to have a child out of wedlock, and I remember discussing it with James back when we started living together, and we both agreed that it was best to wait until we got married to start a family.

Speaking of James, I received a call from him a couple of weeks after the wedding. He called to congratulate me. He said he heard that I had gotten married, and he was happy for me. We made small talk for a minute; he said that he had settled in, the job was great, and he was glad he made the move. I wished him continued success, and he wished me the same, and we hung up. I was surprised to have heard from him. After he left, he had called one time, and it wasn't so much about talking to me personally but about me looking for a receipt he might have left in the apartment when he moved. I didn't find it; it could have been in the stuff he took to his parents' home.

"Tony, I called to him from the bathroom, "come and look at this."

I had bought the pregnancy test kit, and I waited till after we had put Ezra to bed, and just before I took my shower, I followed the instructions and did the test.

"What are you doing?" he asked.

"I took this pregnancy test, and it looks positive."

"Let me see." He took the tester from me and compared it to the examples on the box.

"According this, you are pregnant. Sweetheart, this is wonderful, but we are going to have to make sure. How soon do you think you will be able to get a doctor's appointment?"

"I'll call Dr. Phillips tomorrow. I am sure he may be able to fit me in. At worst, it would probably be the next day. I think I definitely will try to see him tomorrow because I have this cramping feeling as if my periods are coming."

"You know something, you probably are pregnant. Remember yesterday morning, I felt so nauseous? I was thinking about it, and it took me back to when Robin became pregnant with Ezra. You know they say that some men experience morning sickness when their wife becomes pregnant."

"I didn't know that. I thought only the woman went through morning sickness. This should be interesting, both of us sick in the morning— that will be no fun."

"That's for sure. After the two times I was sick when she was expecting with Ezra, I didn't experience again. I have to wait and see how this pregnancy will affect me. I don't mind suffering along with you. I enjoyed it along with you to get you there, so I could go all the way with it. This is my love baby," he said, bending his head to kiss my belly. "I hope it's a girl."

"Me too. I always said I wanted a little girl to dress up and put pretty ribbons in her hair."

"Tomorrow, call Dr. Phillips, and if you can get an appointment to see him, call me and let me know what time. I may be able to meet you there."

"OK," I said, "I will call as soon as I believe he is in. Let me take my shower and get some rest."

"I am coming in with you. I have to protect you and make sure you don't slip or anything. I have to take care of my two girls, you and her—we have to give her name soon," he said, smiling from ear to ear.

We took our shower and went off to bed, Tony hugging me close as we settled in and kissing my back as we drifted off to sleep.

The next morning, I called the doctor's office about ten o'clock, and the receptionist said she may be able to fit me in about 2:30 p.m. I called Tony, and he said he would try to make it over there. He was in lower Manhattan on an audit. My doctor was on Seventh Avenue, just off of Flatbush, around the Grand Army Plaza area. Tony said he would get on the train and meet me there.

I arrived at two thirty, as was the appointment. I asked Steven for the rest of the evening off. It didn't make sense to try to go back to work after the doctor. Sometimes you have to wait longer in the office, so chances are by the time I get through, it will probably be close to 4:00 p.m. It would make no sense to get back to the office and just turn around to go home. Steven didn't have a problem with me leaving early, so off I went.

I called Tony and told him I was on my way. He said he was wrapping up what he was working on and would leave in another fifteen minutes.

As it turned out, there was one person ahead of me, and just as the nurse called me in, Tony walked in. The nurse told him, after the examination, she will call him in so we can both speak to the doctor.

The doctor gave me a urine test and took a blood sample to send to the lab. I told him about the cramping feeling that I was experiencing at intervals. He asked me if I had any spotting, and I told him no. After the examination, I went into his office, and the nurse showed Tony into the room.

"Congratulations, Mr. and Mrs. Bradley, we are pregnant," Dr. Phillips said with a smile on his face.

Tony reached over from his chair and hugged me; this was a moment of pure joy for me. I had never heard those words before.

"Now, Maureen, we will get started on your prenatal care right away. If the cramp continues into next week, let me know, as I may have to order a sonogram just to make sure all is well. If you have any concerns, please don't hesitate to call me right away."

"Thank you, Dr. Phillips," I said. "I will call."

"Thank you, Dr. Phillips," Tony said, extending his hand to shake the doctor's hand.

We left the office floating on a cloud. Once outside, Tony just hugged me.

"Oh, don't let me hug you too tight. I don't want to squeeze our baby."

"Oh, you can hug me," I replied. "You are not going to hurt her or me. You know I live on your hugs."

"Yes, Mommy!" he said. "Let's go home and celebrate. I am cooking you a special dinner tonight. I have to make sure you are strengthened up. You have at least another eight months to go."

We got on the Flatbush Avenue bus and transferred downtown for the C train home. Once at home, he told me to relax, and he proceeded to cook a fish soup, Jamaican style, it was quite tasty.

We decided that we will share the news on Sunday when we go to church. I figure I will wait till then to tell Mom also.

The rest of the week went by uneventful. On Saturday evening, I didn't feel well. Tony was concerned, and I assured him that I will be all right. We decided not to go to church on Sunday, as I really was not feeling that great. He felt that I should take it easy, and of course, he wouldn't leave me alone to go to church.

Aunt Mae picked up Ezra to take him to Sunday school and church with her. I spent most of the day resting.

On Monday morning, I felt good enough to go to work. For the next two days, I felt OK.

On Thursday, I worked without any cramping. However, once I got home, the cramping started. It was severe so I decided that I would call Dr. Phillips in the morning and let him know how I have been feeling.

I didn't eat any dinner, just had a cup of tea, and I retired early. Tony took care of Ezra and finally put him to bed.

When he came to bed, he was concerned, and I could tell he was worried. I tried to make light of it, and I told him that sometimes women have rough pregnancies at the beginning, but I will be all right. We retired as usual for the night. I didn't want to take any over-the-counter remedy for the pain, so I tried to relax, and eventually, I drifted off to sleep.

Sometime in the early morning hours I was awoken suddenly by a sharp pain in my belly. I turned over in bed and touched Tony, and he sat up instantly.

"What's the matter?" he asked.

"I have a bad pain in my belly," I replied.

"You think I should try calling the doctor?" he asked. I could see that he was alarmed.

"I am sure he would say if it's severe, I should go to the emergency room".

I realized that it was three o'clock in the morning, I walked into the bathroom and checked my underwear there was no bleeding.

My belly, however, felt very tender. I came back into the bedroom; the pain was intensifying.

"Tony, I think I better go to the hospital. Something is not right. The pain is getting worse."

"OK, I am calling 911," he said as he picked up the phone.

I touched my belly; it seemed a little swollen. I was trying not to panic, but I was in pain. I heard him giving the operator all the information. He hung up and called Aunt Mae, telling her to come over right away, to stay with Ezra as he has to rush me to the hospital.

He helped me put on a dress, and I pushed my feet in a pair of slippers. He hurriedly got dressed, and holding on to me, we went downstairs. Aunt Mae had arrived and let herself in.

"Tony, Maureen, what's going on?" Aunt Mae asked, seeing the condition I was in. I could see that she had jumped out of bed upon receiving the call. She had hastily put a dress over her nightgown, her head stilled tied with a scarf, and the sleep still in her face.

"We don't know. She may be having a miscarriage," Tony answered. I have called the ambulance. Stay with Ezra, and I will call you to let you know what is going on. Call Mom and tell her we are on our way to the hospital."

EMS arrived at the door, and Tony let them in. They put me in a chair and placed me in the ambulance. They took me to Interfaith Hospital on Atlantic Avenue. By the time they rolled me into the ER, I was in severe pain; my belly looked even more swollen. I started crying and groaning, I held on to Tony's hand tightly. Tony answered most of the questions for the triage nurse.

A doctor came and started examining me. Tony told him that we just found out a week ago that I was pregnant. He finished the examination and said he will be right back.

"Tony, oh god, this is bad, this pain is bad," I said, my mind trying to understand what was going on.

I knew that this pregnancy was ended. Something was happening, and whatever it was, it was not good.

"Hold on, baby, the doctor is coming right back," he said.

I saw him leave the area they had me in, and I could hear him talking to the nurse. He was asking her if she had an idea what could be happening. I heard the nurse tell him that the sonogram technician is on his way. The doctor ordered a vaginal sonogram to see what's happening.

He came back into room and told me that they ordered a sonogram for me. A few minutes later, the technician appeared and did the procedure. Tony waited outside for him to complete it. He left, and I could feel my belly getting big. I felt as if my eyes were popping out my head, and I had this tension headache; my ears felt stuffed. I remember hearing something about getting me to the OR stat. I felt myself being pushed, and I looked and I saw Tony walking beside the gurney. When I looked again, I didn't see him, and I felt the mask go over my face, and I remember nothing else.

As I opened my eyes, my mind slowly began to remember that I was in the hospital. I could feel something in my mouth. I tried moving my hand, but they were strapped to the bed. My eyes focused, and I saw Tony standing over me. He was trying so hard to be brave, but I could see concern written all over his face.

"Sweetheart, try to stay calm. Your hands are strapped to the bed because they had to intubate you. You had an ectopic pregnancy. I don't want you to worry about anything. You are going to be fine. I am not leaving you. The doctor says they will extubate you shortly. Try not to think about the machine. I will ask the nurse if they can release your hands."

He left for a minute and returned with the nurse, who untied my hands, and he held on to one of them.

"Sweetheart, your mom and my mom are outside waiting. They want to come and see you. I am going to go and let them come in for a few minutes, OK?"

I held his hand, and in his palm, I spelled out "OK." He smiled, and he left.

A few minutes later, Mom and Marion appeared, holding on to each other. They tried their best to smile, but I know my mom so well; she was struggling so hard to be brave. She and Marion came over and kissed me on the forehead.

Marion said, "We love you, Maureen, and we are praying for you, but I know that God has already given us the victory."

I reached up and took Marion's hand. I wrote on her palm "sing." I needed to hear something to distract me from the tube down my throat and the machine that was breathing for me. I didn't want to going into a full-blown panic attack.

"What do want to hear?" she started to say but changed her mind and said, "I am going to sing you a happy song because we serve an awesome God."

She sang the words to a chorus, "It's all right, all right, it is all right, all right as long as I have my Lord beside me, it is all right." Marion has a lovely voice, and she sang it just for me to hear.

"They told us we could only spend five minutes, so we are going to leave so Tony can come back in."

I held out my hand to my mom, and she took it and kissed it. "Your father is outside too. He'll come and see you a little later."

They left, and Tony came back in. His eyes appeared a little red; I felt he must have been crying. He tried his best to keep a smile on his face. He told me that the doctor said they should be extubating me shortly.

About ten minutes later, a lady showed up; she was the respiratory therapist. Tony was asked to step out for a minute, and she proceeded to remove the tube from my mouth.

From the recovery room, I was taken up to the fourth floor and placed in a room. Tony accompanied me on the elevator and waited outside the room until I was settled inside.

I know that he was exhausted; this whole event had taken a toll on him.

"Sweetheart, your mom, dad, and your brother want to come up, so I am going to run home and check on Aunt Mae and Ezra and come right back while they visit with you. The doctor says you should be able to go home by Sunday."

"All right. Kiss Ezra for me," I said softly. He kissed me on the lips, and he left. I lay there thinking. I looked at the IV in my hand, and the line led to the unit of blood they had hooked up to the pole, plus another bag of liquid that was all running through the IV. I had an ectopic pregnancy, which meant the fetus was developing in my fallopian tube. that meant that I lost the pregnancy and the tube.

As I was thinking, Mom, Dad, and Charlie appeared in the doorway. Dad and Charlie came up and kissed me, trying their best to smile, but I know that once they heard what went on, they knew that I had been at death's door. Mom came and took my hand.

"I heard you will be home by Sunday. If you want, I will come over to help you with anything you need."

"Thanks, Mom. Whatever you want to do, I am just thanking God right now for my life."

"Anyway, darling," Mom said, "don't talk too much and stress yourself. Everything is going to be fine. I love you, baby."

They sat with me for the next ten minutes, and Mom received a call, and it was Marion saying that she and Pastor were downstairs waiting to come up, as only three people were allowed at a time. Dad and Charlie said that they will go down so that the others could come up.

Pastor and Marion came up and visited with me. Just before they left, Pastor, Marion, and Mom joined hands and prayed for me. I know the tears were running down my face. Mom took a tissue and wiped my eyes.

"Maureen," she said, "don't worry about anything. You are going to be fine. When you come home in a few days, we will talk. Try to rest. I am staying until Tony comes back."

"OK, Mom," I said, and I closed my eyes.

I could feel the tears running from my eyes, try as I may the thought that I lost my baby played over in my mind.

Chapter 24

Two months had gone by since my emergency surgery. As I suspected, I lost one tube and the baby. I spent three days in the hospital, and I had two weeks home to recover. The whole experience left me a bit shaken. When I listened to accounts of the emergency given to me by Tony, my mom, and Marion, I knew I was lucky. Tony said that I started to go into shock and that when the nurses and doctor mobilized and rushed me off to surgery, I was hemorrhaging internally.

He said that my parents and his parents showed up during the time I was in surgery. He said that it felt like an eternity waiting for word that the surgery was completed. He said that while waiting Marion called several members of her prayer group and had everyone praying for me.

He also said that during that time of waiting, he felt like he couldn't exhale. He said that he prayed continuously because if he didn't, he had no idea how he would have survived without me.

Tony took three days off after I came home and won't let me do anything. I could only get up to go to the bathroom and sit in the living room as a break from being in the bedroom all the time.

Mom also came over several days during that time to assist with anything that was to be done. Of course, Aunt Mae was here taking care of Ezra.

Ezra came to give me a kiss every morning, and he would ask, "Are you OK, Mommy?" I told him I was OK and I will be up and around in a few days.

Once I started moving around much better, Mom looked so relieved.

As we sat in the living room, she said to me, "Maureen, I was never so scared in my life. When I walked into that recovery room and saw you lying on that bed, it didn't even look like you. Your face was swollen, the tubing down your throat, and the unit of blood in the IV, it took all my willpower not to scream the place down.

It was as if I had a flashback to the day your grandmother died and I went up in the ICU and saw her on the respirator. I knew that if I showed my feeling, it would have alarmed you, and I didn't want that. But girl, once I got back outside, I lost it. I started crying. I made Tony cry. I think he was trying so hard to hold it together, but once I broke down, it pushed him over the edge.

He came up to me and hugged me, and he said,

'Mom, I know how you feel. It doesn't look like her, does it? The doctor says she will be all right. They took care of everything. She is young and healthy. She will be all right.'

I was a mess. Marion was a tower of strength for us. That woman could pray. She prayed with me and your father, and it really made me feel better, and I believed her when she said that we have claimed the victory in the precious name of Jesus."

"Mom, I was unaware of all that went on, but I know that once I came to, that if Tony wasn't there, I would have probably freaked out. That tube in my mouth, my hands strapped down and being unable to talk, it was the most frightening thing I ever experienced.

I know that once Tony was there, he was going to leave no stone unturned to make sure I was taken care of. You know, Mom, what if I didn't take the chance and get back with him, who is to say what my life would be like? I took the chance, and I don't regret it. I am sorry I lost my baby, but Tony said the doctor said my other tube is healthy, and there is no reason why I can't get pregnant."

"You will have your baby. Just give your body and your mind time to heal," she said. "I know that this was a traumatic experience for you. I understand you had to be given six units of blood because you had lost so much blood. Maureen, you are blessed to be alive. God was on your side to pull you through."

"I truly feel blessed. The outpouring of prayers and the calls I have received show me how much people cared."

"Girl," Mom continued, "I forgot to tell you, when I called Lisa to tell her what happened to you, she started bawling and crying on the phone. I had to try to calm her down, and I told her if she wanted to come to the hospital to see you, she can't cry. I told her I will keep her posted, and maybe it would be better if she waits until you come home to come and visit you. She said OK."

"She came the day after I came home from the hospital, and she was all smiles and said she was happy I was home. I know she was working hard to keep her composure. She is tough on the outside but very sensitive on the inside, and I know she would have lost it over me."

"That's for sure, Mom said with a smile, that why she's your BFF.

Marion came by also, and she too spent some time with me. Sometimes, people say so much negative things about mothers-in-law, and while everyone may have their experiences, I know that Marion loves me.

From the first day she met me until now, she had shown me love and a caring attitude. I don't know if it's because of all the unfairness I endured at the hands of Robin, or maybe it's because she knows her son loves me and she loves her son and wants the best for him. In any event, she has certainly welcomed me into her family with open arms.

As she sat talking to me, she also relived the event, and she said to me that she cannot even begin to imagine what would have happened to Tony if I had died.

"Maureen," she said, "every day I just praise God for sparing your life. I took Tony home after we left the hospital that first day, and he just broke down.

He said to me,

"Mom, I almost lost her. I just got her, and I almost lost her."

"I told him that our God is in charge of all things, and he has the plan for our lives. I prayed with him, and I told him he has to stay strong for you and for Ezra because both of you are depending on him.

It's just that he loves you so much, and he has been through so much already, and now he is finally settling into the life he wanted, and this happened—it really shook him up."

"Marion, I know it was tough for him. It was as if a couple of days before, we got the good news, and days later, I am fighting for my life. I know he loves me, I have no doubt whatsoever, and I love him just the same, and I pray that God will grant us a long life together. We are taking it one day at a time, and we know that we have each other's back."

Two weeks later, I went back to work, and slowly our lives went back to normal. Tony and I decided to use an alternative method of birth control, as I did not want to go back on the pill, and I wanted my body to heal and get back to a natural rhythm. I changed my GYN doctor. I had been a patient of Dr. Phillips for a while, and I know it wasn't entirely his fault, but I think once I told him about the cramping, he should have looked into it right away. Chances are I would have still lost the baby, but I would have been spared the ordeal that I went through.

When we decide that we will try again, I want to be sure that I am taken care of completely. I don't want to take a chance on losing my only good tube that is left.

Gloria recommended her doctor who delivered her girls, and I decided that I will make an appointment for my yearly GYN check, and that way, it would give me a chance to meet him and see if we could be a fit.

The first Sunday I attended church services after my illness, I received so many hugs, and many of the sisters and brothers were glad to see me out. I was glad to be out and to give God praise and thanks for saving my life.

November rolled around, and so did my birthday, the big 3 0. I was happy to celebrate it. That Sunday in church, when Pastor Bradley did an altar call, I seem to be propelled out my chair, and I walked up to the front and gave my life to God. I had felt the calling from the first day I went to the church, but at that time, I was so confused. My life back then was in such turmoil.

Today, I no longer felt that way. My life has been changed from one of uncertainty and frustration to one of happiness and a thankful heart. I have been blessed with a husband and son that loves me, my family, and my extended family who care so much for me.

When I walked up to the front, I could see the smile on Pastor Bradley's face. Marion came up to me and put her arms around me and hugged me. The way the choir sang, the way Pastor Bradley prayed, I felt as if the Holy Spirit of God surrounded me, and I broke down and cried with Marion still holding on to me.

At the end, Tony came up and escorted me back to my seat, holding my hand as we sat down.

I had now become a candidate for baptism. According to the church custom, baptismal class were held for three months, giving the candidates time to begin to study the word of God and see if you are committed to be in the service of God. I attended classes cheerfully every week for the three-month period, and finally, on the second Sunday in February 2011, I was baptized. After the service, which was attended by my parents and Lisa, we all went over to Marion's for lunch. It was a joyous occasion, a beginning of my life for the Lord.

I know Tony was elated; he had given his life to God a long time ago, and now without even asking me to do so, I came to God of my own free will. There is a hymn that says, "When I think of the goodness of Jesus and what he has done for me, my soul cries out Hallelujah thank God for saving me."

As I think back on my life, I could see how God has been there for me on so many occasions even though I didn't know it. Yes, I have had my share of trials and heartaches; but through it all, he has given me the strength and the courage to make it. I realize that if we could only place our lives in God's hands and trust that he has our best interest at heart, we could save ourselves a lot of grief.

June 2011, I heard those wonderful words again, "Congratulation, Mrs. Bradley, you are pregnant." Right away, Dr. Weitz ordered a sonogram to make sure the fetus was in the right place and everything was in order. Tony and I discussed whether we wanted to know the sex of the baby. We decided that we didn't want to know, we were going to do it the old-fashioned way and be happy with whatever God gives us. All we want is a healthy baby. Surprising enough, Tony had no morning sickness like he did the last time. As to whether he really had it or not, we'll never know.

At first, I didn't really get morning sickness per se, but by the sixth week, I could not take the smell of some foods, and the smell of raw chicken sent me scurrying to the bathroom. Eventually, my stomach settled, and I was able to eat a lot better.

The first time the doctor let me hear the heartbeat, I was so happy. Not to mention, the first time the baby moved, I called Tony so he could put his hand and feel the movement. Both of our families were excited, but no one was more excited than Mom. This was her first grandchild, and already she was talking about my coming over to the house after the baby is born so she can help me. I told her to let me have the baby first, and we will decide if I want to come there after the birth or have her come over and spend a few days to help me out.

As we awaited the delivery, the guest room was changed into the nursery. We held off on buying the cradle until after the birth, but Marion got us a bassinette on wheels with a multicolor canopy. It was cute.

Between Mom, Marion, and Lisa, they planned a baby shower, which was held that February, a month before my due date. I personally think that it was an excuse for them to have a party.

It was held at Mom's house, and they cooked up a storm. I was surprised to see so many guys accompanying their girlfriends or wives to the shower. We played music, open the gifts and feasted on all the good food that had been cooked. We enjoyed the evening.

Lisa bought me a stroller with the detached car seat. She will be one of the godmothers, of course. We received baby clothes of all colors and sizes, bottles, gift cards, toys, and money; it. Tony and myself thanked everyone for their support, love and gifts.

As the days roll by, I took it all in stride. I prayed daily and asked God to grant me safe delivery, thanking him always for all that he had done and is doing for me.

Tony couldn't wait for our bundle of joy to arrive. He had it all worked out. He tried to plan what would happen if he was at work when I go into labor and how much time it would take him to get to the hospital if he were in the city. He hoped it would happen when he was at home, but he knew with babies, you cannot make any plans; they come when they are ready.

I decided I was going to work as long as I could before the birth and take as much time as I could at home after the birth. My due date was March 19, but as the doctor said, it could be before that date as well as it could be after.

Tony felt that I shouldn't push myself and suggested that I make March 9, which was a Friday, my last day at work, that would give me at least a week to relax and prepare. I discussed it with Steven, and he did not have a problem, so we settled on that date.

With all the things we were doing and thinking about, we still had not decided on a name. Since we did not know the sex of the baby, we had to select a boy and a girl name. We considered Travis, Jayden, and Michael for a boy; and if it was a girl, Jordan, Kayla, or Alexis. I personally love the name Jordan for a girl.

Tony had his reservations about that one, and we said we will think about it some more. My first two days home were great; it gave me the opportunity to put away the baby clothes in the chest of drawers we bought for the room and just put things in place. I designated a cupboard in the kitchen for all the baby bottles and utensils. I know I will need them at some point, but I planned to breast-feed my baby for the first two months at least.

That Wednesday morning, I woke up with a dull pain in my back. I mentioned it to Tony. At that point, he said he was not going to work because if the baby was on its way, he needed to be here. I started to tell him that they say first delivery takes longer, so the baby may not get there until tonight.

He said, "Whenever he or she gets there, I am going to be there. I already put the job on notice that I have to be there when my wife gives birth to our child."

Over the next two hours, the pain started to intensify, and I called Dr. Weitz. He told us to make our way over to the hospital, and he will be in shortly. He was affiliated with Brooklyn Hospital, and we got dressed, picked up my overnight bag that I had packed, and drove over to the hospital.

We went to Labor and Delivery as instructed by Dr. Weitz, and they set me up in a room. Dr. Weitz came about an hour later, examined me, and confirmed that I was in labor. During the examination, my water broke, and to me, that was confirmation that I was having the baby today. I was hooked up to a monitor, and for a minute, I was relaxed enough. I drifted off into a light nap.

Tony, in the meantime, called my mom and his mom and Aunt Mae so she will know that she will have to stay with Ezra this evening.

Over the next three hours, the pain continued, my contractions were getting closer, and they kept checking as to how much I had dilated. I had said I was going to avoid taking any drug during labor, but as the pain got worse, I asked the doctor for something to help ease the pain. He gave me epidural, and that helped a little.

At least another hour went by, and then I could feel myself wanting to push. They took me from that room and carried into a delivery room. Tony had to put on a gown, and he held on to my hand. As Dr. Weitz would tell me to "breathe" then "push," Tony was telling me, "You can do it, baby." One last push, and I heard the cry of that little voice.

"It's a girl," Dr. Weitz said, all excited. "Congratulations, you have a beautiful baby girl."

They cleaned her up and put her on my chest. I felt the tears starting to run down my cheeks. I looked at Tony; he was smiling but also wiping a tear from his eye.

"I love you, baby," he said, "always did, always will."

I placed my hand around my little girl. *Thank you, Father God,* I prayed silently, and as I prayed, something said to me, "Her name is Faith."

"Tony," I said, her name is Faith."

"Praise God," he said, it's beautiful, just like her, just like you."

"I love you, sweetheart," I said.

Once everything was done, the baby was sent up to the nursery, and I went up to a room on the maternity floor.

Later that evening, Mom and Dad, Marion and Pastor, came to visit me and to see the baby. By the end of the evening, my room was full of flowers. As I looked at them, I felt like a woman who was truly loved by her husband, her family, and so many well-wishers. Sometimes we never know the impact we leave on people's lives; and really, it's just about the way we treat each other.

As beautiful as the flowers were, I told Tony to take some of them home when he was leaving. Once my visitors left, they brought Faith from the nursery. Tony sat on the edge of the bed close to me.

"Sweetheart," he said, "do you need anything before I leave? I hate to leave, but I have to see about Ezra and give Aunt Mae a break. Have you decided what will be her middle name?"

"Antonia, Faith Antonia Bradley," I said, happiness bursting through my being, my little girl finally here.

"A big name for such a small girl," he said with a smile, "but she will grow into it."

He reached over and kissed her little head, and then he kissed me. "My queen and my princess," he said, "I love you both so much."

Maybe it was my imagination, but for the first time, in a long time, his eyes shone with such happiness; it was as if I could see all the love and happiness that he had hoped for finally fulfilled. It was as if light had returned to his being, and it made its presence known by the sparkle in his eyes.

We sat watching her little form. She was so beautiful, those tiny hands and feet; for the first time as we watched her, she opened her eyes, and I looked at Tony, and I smiled because those eyes that were looking at us were his eyes.

About the Author

MW Dacosta (Marcia) lives in Brooklyn NY. Originally, from the beautiful island of Barbados, she has lived most of her adult life in Brooklyn. This is her second novel; of three novels she has written with the theme of 'Love Forever.'

The first novel is titled 'Journey into Forever'. And the third novel is titled 'Forever isn't Long Enough to Love You'

In Forever My Love, the story of Tony and Maureen is told with a flavor that's all Brooklyn, but with a touch of the Islands. Many of the old adages that Marcia grew up hearing from her mother and others have been incorporated into the story, to weave a tale of treachery and deceit that is conquered by true love. *Forever My Love* reminds us that true love has the power to correct all wrongs, take us through the darkest of times and bring us to that place of beauty and joy forever.

www.ingramcontent.com/pod-product-compliance
Lightning Source LLC
Chambersburg PA
CBHW031527310726
48971CB00008B/2375